minding

CHRIS PALING is the author of seven previous novels.
He is married with two children and lives in Brighton.

By the same author

From the reviews of Chris Paling's previous novels

After the Raid:

'Haunting, intense and enviably accomplished.' **Nick Hornby**

'A complex moral fable as well as a meticulous psychological study.' **Giles Foden, TLS**

'An impressive feat of historical imagining.' **Jason Cowley, Independent**

'The creation of suspense through such laconic writing reminds one of Graham Greene.' **Literary Review**

Morning All Day:

'It is a rare book that can bring a reader close to tears, but *Morning All Day* becomes one of them.' **Guardian**

'Sharply observed and bleakly funny.' **D J Taylor, Mail on Sunday**

'A witty and harrowing account of love, marriage and mid-life crises... [Paling] refuses to opt for relentless misery, concentrating instead on creating a series of wry, acutely observed vignettes that elicit as many laughs as winces.' **Harry Ritchie, The Times**

'Swiftly and realistically rendered... Paling examines the psychology of his characters with humane but unflinching determination. His own instinct for the fundamental truths of human nature, and his commitment to their examination in this engrossing, compassionate novel, are admirable.' **Time Out**

The Silent Sentry:

'Chris Paling is the literary authority on male breakdown and midlife crisis... Paling's sense of humour does remain intact, making sure the effect of the concatenation of disaster is not merely to numb... richly textured.' **Nicholas Royle,** *Independent*

'Chris Paling is a connoisseur of sadness: not simply world-weariness, nor pathological depression, but something approaching "life rage".' *Guardian*

Newton's Swing:

'A small, tense little masterpiece − the sort of emotional thriller that all emotional thrillers should aspire to be.' **Liz Jensen,** *Independent*

'A beautifully crafted murder mystery full of intrigue and suspense. Only a writer of Paling's genius could get away with calling his hero John Wayne.' **Daily Express**

'A subtle study of the anatomy of grief, desire and the father-son relationship.' **Chris Power,** *The Times*

'Paling's novel is not simply a riveting whodunit, but an intelligently dissected study of an emotionally desiccated man.' **Sunday Times**

'Paling is a great thing among British writers: a largely unsung talent who keeps on experimenting.' **Alex Clark,** *Guardian*

'A gripping account of a murder and its aftermath. Paling is a name to watch.' **Observer**

The Repentant Morning:

'Atmospheric and engrossing.' **Shena Mackay**

'Paling is a genuinely unusual kind of a writer, someone who seems to be writing out of what e e cummings called "plain downright honest curiosity: that very greatest of all the virtues". His range is wide... and his style and technique are similarly impressive and wayward... he is formidable.' **Ian Sansom, Observer**

'Paling successfully mixes his ingredients of love, politics and war into a powerful cocktail.' **Sunday Times**

'Steeped in atmosphere, Paling's novel conjures up aspects of 1930s London in a wholly convincing way. His characters are conjured with a sure hand.' **Katie Owen, Sunday Telegraph**

'Intricate and thought-provoking... This is an absorbing, fluently told novel, rich in detail and local colour... but it is the moral ambivalences of war and sexual relations that makes this novel something more than just an adventure story beautifully told.' **Gerard Woodward, Daily Telegraph**

minding | chris paling

Portobello
BOOKS

Published by Portobello Books Ltd 2007

Portobello Books Ltd
Eardley House
4 Uxbridge Street
Notting Hill Gate
London W8 7SY, UK

*A CIP catalogue record is available from
the British Library*

9 8 7 6 5 4 3 2 1

ISBN 1 84627 079 0
13-digit ISBN 978 1 84627 079 6

www.portobellobooks.com

Designed by Lindsay Nash

Typeset in Joanna by Avon DataSet Ltd,
Bidford on Avon, Warwickshire

Printed in the Uk by CPI Bookmarque, Croydon, CR0 4TD

'Fear not: for I have redeemed thee,
I have called thee by thy name; thou art mine.
When thou passest through the waters,
I shall be with thee; and through the rivers,
they shall not overflow thee . . .'

Isaiah

minding

1

The relationship between Jane Hackett and the elderly psychiatrist improved when she stopped challenging his lofty pronouncements. It had taken her some time to accept that to get better you had to give your mind away, or at least temporarily entrust it into someone else's care. And in many ways she preferred him to the others she was obliged to see at the hospital, despite his habit of smelling his fingertips under the pretence of scratching his nose or answering the phone without apology when they were in mid conversation.

But what was it he had just said? Something about life teaching you humility – through illness, friendships, or bearing and raising children. The patient in front of him had, he suggested, through circumstances beyond her control, perhaps learned her lesson too early. There followed a silence which he had expected her to fill, but she hadn't. Two could play at that game.

Jane Hackett's medical notes give her year of birth as 1976. Somewhere, approximately three-quarters of the way down the wad in the thick manila file, is registered the fact that she has one child, a boy, now eleven, whom she now sees only four times a year. What the notes don't record is that Jane has learned not to think about him because to do so makes her sad and angry, both of which emotions she has indulged in to such extremes that they are now considered to be bad for her. What pains her most is when her son's toes come to mind; this one detail of her absent child is what always provokes her to tears. As a result, the manila file contains, in many different inks and hands, details of the drug combinations she has been prescribed to make her feel less sad and angry, a short précis of why they were chosen, and a postscript on their effectiveness. The latest entry concludes with her date of discharge from the hospital which took place a few days after the meeting with the elderly psychiatrist.

For some time following her release Jane was too afraid to face the world. Now she emerges tentatively from her flat for a few hours each day although she tends to stray no more than three or four streets away from her front door. At the moment she is standing outside a tall, narrow, second-hand bookshop, staring in through the window. Despite the decay of the building and the rain cascading onto her head from the blocked guttering, the bookshop is one of her favourite places.

For those prone to making snap judgements, the fact that Jane is wearing no coat and is hugging a large bin bag to her chest, might contribute to making her look like a care-in-the-community case. Jane would hate to be categorized in such a way. She fought very hard for her liberty, eventually achieving it by having proved to a roomful of people that she is sane – or normal – which, she has subsequently worked out, was regarded by them as the same thing. And, despite the bulging bin bag and her saturated dress, Jane looks what most people would consider to be relatively normal. The one false note is the over-formality of her dress. She has three very good fawn rain macs at home (one, an ancient Burberry) but no warm winter coat. She eschews cardigans unless they are unbuttoned and slung around her shoulders, and would prefer to be cold than put on something she didn't think would suit her. Charity-shop clothes look well on her because she is thin. She once had an argument with a woman in a changing room who complimented her on being 'slim'. Jane said it was a stupid term that only women and fashion designers used. Today she wouldn't bother picking a fight over something so trivial; another example, she supposes, of her maintaining at least the pretence of sanity. Jane has straight shoulders and a long delicate neck and sometimes, when she catches sight of her face reflected in a shop window, she imagines she has something of Audrey Hepburn about her, particularly when she has her long, dark hair pinned up. Her eyes, though, tell a different story. While Audrey Hepburn gave the impression of looking on the world as though anything was possible, the intensity of Jane's expression suggests she has learned the hard way what is possible and what is not. She wears what her hospital friend, the Sugar Plum Fairy, identified as a pained smile, delineating, as it does, bravery rather than joy.

Despite everything she has been through, the one thing Jane Hackett has never wished for is to be somebody else. This, at least, was what she announced to the roomful of people at the hospital and she could see some of them smile when she made the remark. She knew the tide was turning in her direction when the woman who had chaired the proceedings reached for a biscuit from the plate on the low table. Removing it broke the precise overlapping circle of digestives. The woman rearranged the remaining ones to fill the gap, but Jane noticed that her anxious eyes continued to return to the plate as if she was afraid she'd be reprimanded for having helped herself. When she caught Jane watching her she sat back, placed the half-eaten biscuit on her right knee, and made a show of becoming engrossed in her notes. That was the moment when Jane knew they would release her.

The morning's rain had provoked a heartfelt apology from the weatherwoman on television. But Jane has never minded the rain or the winter. In many ways she prefers it when the nights draw in because then she doesn't feel guilty about not having anyone to visit. The guilt is rooted in her perception of how other people judge her. If it wasn't for that, she'd be happy to live the life of a hermit.

The bookshop is tall and one room wide and, according to Patrick who runs it, needs twenty-odd grand spending on it. Patrick doesn't own the shop, nor does he work for the man who does. He once explained the arrangement to Jane: how he'd put some money in to secure the 28-year lease, but now couldn't get it back because his partner, Fergal, had thrown a wobbly about it and they had fallen out. Since that time they had come to an agreement over sharing the profits, though Patrick claimed they weren't sufficient for one man to live on, let alone two. But Jane wasn't really listening. Life, she considers, is too short to listen to petty squabbles that don't have any direct bearing on her well-being.

Through the window she can see Patrick behind the counter talking to another man. Jane envies the fact that they seem easy in each other's company because she was only ever easy with her child. She christened him Billy, not William, because she feared it would be shortened. When a woman doctor once suggested to her that Billy's name could, in fact, be shortened, Jane told her it couldn't because she had heard of no boy in recent years ever being called Bill. Very well, the doctor pressed, but perhaps in so naming him she had a premonition that she would one day lose control over him. Jane asked the doctor whether she said such cruel things on purpose – just to provoke a reaction. The doctor countered by suggesting to Jane that perhaps she should examine whether she was being too sensitive. Jane said that, having examined it, she considered she was not –

why did the woman think that? And this was the back-and-forth way in which they talked: in questions that led to suggestions which resulted in more questions that seemed never to be answered. For a long time after she lost Billy, Jane felt that her life was like a wave that was poised but refused to break onto a beach. At least the finger-smelling psychiatrist occasionally said something direct, however misguided or inaccurate it was.

Life is very easy for some people, Jane thinks as she watches Patrick and the man chatting in the shop. Why, nowadays, does she always find it so hard? She opens the door, triggering the bell in its metal apostrophe. Patrick looks towards her, smiles without hesitation, and says, 'Hello, Jane,' and she loves the sound of his voice because he sounds like an old oak tree would if it could talk. His eyes linger on her plastic bag, and his gentle shake of the head is a compliment to her (at least, if you questioned Patrick for a while, that would be the conclusion at which you eventually arrived: a compliment to her individuality). To the other man standing at the counter, however, Patrick's nod looks like a signal to him that a loony has walked into the shop.

Patrick's face is lean, his skin dark, and there's a ploughed field of laughter-lines around his bright eyes. His hair is wiry and prematurely grey. He wears baggy round-necked woollen jumpers, blue Levi's which are tight and faded at the crutch and old, discoloured, Adidas trainers. On the occasions Jane has tried to assess whether or not Patrick has a good physique she usually concludes that although he isn't particularly fat, neither would he amount to much if he stood in front of her naked. He'd probably have curly grey hairs on his chest and around his small willy.

Jane doesn't echo Patrick's greeting. She tends only to speak when they are alone in the shop. Patrick places a paperback book in a brown paper bag far too big for it (a job lot from the wholesalers), folds the bag in half, and hands it reluctantly to the customer. Fergal once despairingly commented that you could be forgiven for thinking that each book Patrick sold was the gem of his own private collection. Jane recognizes the customer as one of the regulars; a furtive man who visits the shop for the company but often leaves having bought a book on military history. ('You wouldn't like to know what was on his hard drive, now would you, Jane?' Patrick commented once, and she'd pretended to know what he had meant.)

Jane goes past the men, stilled and silenced by her proximity, puts her bag behind the counter without seeking Patrick's permission, and climbs a set of narrow, dark stairs (on which books are stacked on each uncarpeted tread) to a room at the top marked: Classics, Biographies, Plays, Children's. This room is crammed (on the thin shelves, on the bare floor) with paperbacks and hardbacks; piles of leather-bound copies of Punch are stacked on the bowed floorboards.

Jane goes immediately to the Classics' section and searches along the rows of black-spined Penguins. She looks up and down, left to right, becoming more fractious. Then, from a shelf above her head, she pulls out a paperback and holds it to her heart, breathing more easily again.

Downstairs, Patrick, now alone in the shop, is watching her on an old black and white TV which is rigged up to the CCTV. He is drinking cold, sweet tea from a mug with the name of a double-glazing company on it: Bishop's. Patrick's day is measured out in cups of tea and coffee: six in the morning, five in the afternoon; an alcoholic in every respect but the alcohol. He sees Jane walk towards the camera, the book against her chest, and he watches her pause and smile up towards him as she always does. When she passes beneath the camera he glimpses her sharp parting, glossed by the fluorescent light, and then hears her tread immediately upon the stairs.

When Patrick takes the book from her it's a tender gesture. In the moment they both have hold of it a blush of feeling flows between them through the pages. Patrick looks at Jane, reading her for a while. But, as always, she is unreadable. She continues to stare at the book in his hand. The book is Guy de Maupassant's *Pierre et Jean*.

Patrick says: 'Are you well today, Jane, given the inclemency of the weather?' His voice is gluey from the tea in his throat.

But she's now engaged in looking at the photographs on the wall behind him. There are hundreds of these orphaned bookmarks pinned up on the damp plaster. The gold of many of the pin-heads is rusty.

It no longer concerns Patrick that he has to go along with

Jane at her own speed. The kettle is boiling again on the shelf beneath the counter, at groin level. He leans down and pours the water into a mug, drops in a bag of strawberry tea, and hands the cup to Jane. She takes it without thanks. The bag bleeds slowly into the water and the medicinal smell of the fruit floods the moist air around them.

'I thought you'd given up on me.' When all else fails, Patrick knows that something in Jane responds to flirtation, even when she has tuned everything else out.

'Why? Why did you think that?'

'Well, you haven't been to see me for a couple of weeks.'

'No. That's good isn't it: two weeks?'

'Good?'

'Yes, it was hard not to come.'

'OK.'

Jane watches Patrick try to puzzle this one out, but he can't, so he asks her, 'So what have you been doing with yourself?'

'This and that.'

'I thought I might take a break: a few days away. Shut up the shop. Go and see the old folks.' Patrick offers up the thought for debate. He wants Jane to talk him out of it. He can usually count on her insecurities to furnish him with reasons not to visit Dún Laoghaire but today she isn't interested in his old folks.

'That's new,' she says of one of the photographs on the wall behind him. Patrick reaches to unpin it. He knows the layout of his photo-gallery so well that he almost doesn't need to turn and look.

The photograph shows the head of a sun-tanned woman in a Stetson. Her face has the definition of a model; her cheekbones are prominent and the camera has caught her at an unguarded moment, just as she has turned to face the photographer. The expression of shocked delight is genuine.

Patrick says: 'Page 36, Proust 1. *Penguin 20th Century Classics*. Personally I've never made it past page 5 of the Overture.'

On the photo is a small, yellow Post-it note.

'What does it say on that yellow sticky?' Jane asks him.

'"Smoking is keen – Smoking is cool – Smoking is good." In pencil, soft pencil. Well?'

Jane holds out her hand and Patrick passes the photograph to her. Jane contemplates it for a moment and then she says, 'Lover.'

'Do you think so?'

Jane continues to look at it and says, 'Yes. Lover.'

'I thought it might be the wife . . .'

Jane hands the photograph back to Patrick who studies it briefly before pinning it beneath a piece of card on which, in blue ink, he has written 'Lover'. His bookmark gallery is categorized under the headings 'Spouse', 'Child', 'Lover', 'Family', 'Friend', 'Associate', 'Enemy', 'Other'. The photos overlap.

'Perhaps you're right,' Patrick says, assessing the new position. 'Lover.' He waits for Jane to comment but she doesn't. '. . . So, Jane, what does the day have in store for you?' Patrick can imagine a world for most of his customers, even for those he would prefer not to know. But Jane has always proved a challenge to him, so much so that he now thinks of her as a ghost who ceases to exist when she leaves his premises.

'I'm going to the launderette.'

'I see,' Patrick says, bereft of opinion. 'That'll just be a pound, then.'

Jane opens her small purse, pinches out a coin like a child with toy money and hands it to Patrick who takes it and puts it into the drawer he uses for a till. Jane watches her pound until the drawer is shut and the coin is locked away in the darkness.

'Bring it back when you've read it and I'll buy it back from you if you like,' Patrick says as if it's an old joke. But it's not a joke to Jane. When she does bring the book back to Patrick it's a huge effort to entrust it into his care. She doesn't like abandoning anything. This was what she meant when she told him it was hard for her not to come and see him for two weeks. It disappoints her when people don't understand her, but it no longer worries her that the way her mind works seems to be so different from the way everyone else's works. Jane's chain of thought, at this point, goes like this:

stayawayfortwoweeks/havingtoexplaintoPatrickwhatthat means/hedoesn'tunderstand/thinkdifferentlytoPatrickand everybodyexceptthepeopleinthehospital/sometimesIcantalk tothem/weallliketheapplepieinthere.

Patrick watches Jane manoeuvre her bin bag through the narrow door and out into the rain soaked street. Her

11

presence lingers in the shop until he begins to roll a cigarette. The act of mild concentration demanded by this cleanses her from his mind.

It is still raining hard. Jane puts the brown paper bag against her breasts and anchors it behind the bin bag to protect it from the rain. Her hair is saturated, as are the shoulders of her dress.

2

The greenhouse humidity of the launderette warms her but does not dry her clothes. Jane sits on the flimsy, plastic chair beneath the electric clock watching, but not seeing, her clothes churn in the dryer. Beside her, a feral boy in a grey, hooded sweatshirt is talking to his mate on a minuscule mobile phone. A radio plays in the small back office where a Bengali woman takes in the service washes. The woman is leaning on the shelf of her stable-door, smiling at the cheerful banalities of the DJ. Jane has an empty carrier bag at her feet. She is princess of the small space around her. Her brown paper bag is on her knee. She takes out the paperback book and opens it. On the title page is an inscription, written in fountain pen ink: 'To Jane. With all my love (there is no more to be had)'. The letters are small and slant slightly to the left. Jane runs her fingers over the inscription then closes the book and puts it face down onto her knee, her palm resting lightly against it. She continues to sit straight-backed, watching the machine and listening to the boy ranting into his phone.

'If I see cun' ag'in, I ain' gonna speak to 'im,' Scott, inside the priest's cowl of his hoodie, tells his phone as Jane looks back towards the clothes in the dryer, circling like the fanlight in her bedroom.

The fanlight rattles. Jane keeps the vent open because the room is damp. It's a poor flat, but it is clean. Cleanliness, to Jane, represents safety. When the stern man and woman visited her and she wasn't coping, one of the reasons they gave for taking away her child was the filth in her flat. Jane argued that it wasn't filth, it was just mess, but they didn't accept the distinction. And they said it wasn't the first time, which seemed to make it a worse crime.

She is lying under a thick duvet listening to the voice of Maria Callas coming through the wall. It feeds her heart. A hot-water bottle lies on her chest, the approximate mass and weight of a damp, sleeping baby. She never minded the smell of Billy's wee – it wasn't horrible, like mens', it was pure, like apple juice. It wouldn't have repulsed her to drink a cup of it. You wouldn't have had to have offered her a thousand pounds, or even ten. She'd have drunk it gratefully for free.

Jane extends a naked arm from the covers into the chill of the room to pick up the paperback book from her bedside table. She then stretches both of her arms high above her face, opens the book and begins to read. A photo falls from the pages and butterflies onto her chest. She lays down the book, picks up the photograph and looks at it: a young man wearing baggy jeans and no shirt, visible ribs, with a boy's untainted smile. The photo is torn in half. A woman's slender hand is around the young man's waist. He is standing in a park. Behind him is a stone folly, the pillars of the Greek temple are green with damp and moss. Jane stares at the photo as the music continues through the wall, adding to her welcome melancholy.

'Hello you,' she says to the man.

In her head she hears the sound of his laughter which is abruptly terminated.

Jane gets out of bed swaddled in her duvet and goes to a drawer. She opens it and takes out a drawing-pin. Returning to the bed she pins the photo on the wall above her head – at the centre point where a crucifix would have hung. There is a knock on the door. A reflex makes her check herself; check the room. Is it a mess again? No. Has she gone out again without her clothes on? No. Has she shouted in the library, cried in public or forgotten to pay for her groceries? No. Has she missed an appointment? She looks at the calendar on the wall, blank save for two entries detailing her Friday visits to the hospital. No. The big red circle – the day she next sees Billy – is just over the page, only two weeks away now. Two weeks! She can hardly bear it. If she thinks about it too much she will make herself ill and they won't let her see him, so she tries very hard not to. But so far as she can tell she isn't ill again, so it can't be them coming to fetch her. Nevertheless, she approaches the door tentatively and is relieved when she opens it to find her neighbour, an old man in a rain coat and peaked cap. Alf has reached the age at which he has begun to shrink and his clothes, once snug, are now marginally too large for him. National Service knocked the edges off him when he was an adolescent. It turned him from a shy boy into a man whose character was a troubled mix of arrogance and deference.

'Did you speak to them?' Alf asks her.

Yes, of course, Jane remembers now what this is all about. 'I left a message,' she says.

'What message?'

'I told them we were freezing and we wanted someone to come round and sort it out.'

'Only that's what we pay rent for: room and heating. Did you tell them that?'

'No.'

'I suppose I'd better try them.'

'Yes. You could.'

'They might be more likely to listen to me.'

A door opens along the corridor and the sound of Maria Callas becomes louder. The door closes, and then an elderly woman dressed in a Chinese-patterned silk gown, a silk headscarf over her thin orange hair, comes into Jane's sight.

'Did she speak to them?' the woman asks Alf.

'She left a message.'

'Well that's no good.' The woman makes this accusation

16

towards Jane. Her name is Maude and her voice has the gruff edge of a heavy smoker. She smells of stale cigarette smoke and fresh talcum powder. Maude once confided to Jane that she had made her living in the provincial theatre. Only later did Jane learn she had worked in the box office.

'There was nobody there,' Jane tells her.

'I mean one could perish in this cold – Alf?'

'I'll try them now,' Alf says, weighing the small change in his trouser pocket.

'What did you say to them, dear?' Maude is smiling now. She has remembered that she has decided to be kind to her neighbour. You had to be careful with young women like her because they were the sort who kept everybody up all night with their shouting and screaming when they went off the rails.

'I said I thought the boiler had broken down because we're all freezing to death.'

'Well I hope that does the job.'

'Did you tell them that: "Freezing to death"?' Alf asks her.
'Yes.'

He nods his approval.

'It's really not good enough,' Maude complains to Alf.

'These things happen. So long as they get someone round sharpish to fix it.'

'I have an electric heater,' Maude announces, as if the thought has just occurred to her. 'Except I can't afford to have it on all the time. It eats up the credit on my card like there was no tomorrow.'

'Perhaps we'll come in and share it with you,' Alf offers, winking at Jane.

'You'd be most welcome.'

'No, you're all right, I was only joking,' he says. But Maude has seen a temporary solution to her problems of loneliness and cold.

'Would you like to do that too, dear?' she asks Jane.

'Yes. I would,' Jane replies, not because she wants to but because, faced with the two of them in the enclosed space of the corridor, her free will has become overwhelmed.

'We could have a "do",' Alf suggests. 'I'll bring a couple of bottles of stout round – I've got a steak and kidney pie in a tin. What do you reckon?'

'Well that might be quite nice. Could you bring something, dear?' Maude reasons that if Jane supplies a bottle of wine she might get away with having to provide only the crockery. She hates having to watch every penny but it has now become a way of life.

'Yes, I'll bring something.'

Alf is happy now. As he goes off towards the stairs, his hands deep in his pockets, he calls: 'I'll call them now and report back.'

Jane watches the back of his body disappearing on the stairs like a captain going down with his ship. Maude has vanished silently. There is the sound of voices briefly raised at the far end of the corridor where Frankie lives with Carey and sometimes, at the weekends, the consumptive Afghan boy whom they call 'The Boy'. Jane closes the door on the

18

world, returns to her bed and lies there, staring at the ceiling. Her heart beats fast from the excitement of the contact. The photograph of the young man stares down at her.

The way the photograph has been taken the young man's eyes seem to follow Jane around the room while she dresses for the party. It is now so cold in the flat that her breath shows like tiny white pennants. Opening a cupboard in her kitchenette, she looks in at the meagre fare and wonders what would be appropriate for her visit to Maude's. Removing a small can of ravioli, she puts it on the spotless drainer. The label of the tin is ripped at the point where she tore off the tombola number. She had wanted to win the pink gift-set of powder and perfume and had later seen a child carrying it around the church hall. The child had refused her offer of a pound for it, and Jane had backed away when the girl's mother had shouted at her, assuming a more sinister motive.

Towards the bed she calls: 'Hurry up, we'll be late.' But there is no reply.

In the fridge she finds a half-drunk bottle of rosé wine, some mild, low-fat cheddar, skimmed milk and two sticks of celery. She takes out the wine then she goes back to her drawer for a ribbon. It is the long pink ribbon she kept from the bouquet of carnations *he* once sent her. Jane cuts the ribbon in half with a pair of kitchen scissors, leaves the scissors out on the top of the drawers, returns to the wine and ties the ribbon around it.

Looking around the room again she sees that she has not put the scissors away: mess. So she goes back to the drawer, opens it and puts the scissors inside. The drawer is full of her precious objects: all of them are mementoes of him as well as of all the tender notes he had sent her. When they were together she'd find notes hidden in her room. Once she discovered he had written a message inside the wrapper of a bar of chocolate and had sealed it up again. She found it when she had finished the bar. They were all simple proclamations of love.

Jane closes her eyes, rummages in the drawer and pulls out the small plastic tube left over from the film he had loaded into his new camera ('Snazzy,' he had called it – his camera – and what she loved about him then was that even with his new toy he was still aware of her; she was still the best toy he had). Once, when he made her cry, she held the film container to her cheek and tried to collect her tears in it. When he asked her why she was doing it she told him that she wanted to give him something to remember her by when she was gone; he could put his finger in the tube and taste the salt of her tears. He looked at her as if she was mad.

Why did it frighten him when he saw what was at the edge of her? It didn't mean she couldn't come back from there. It just meant that sometimes she appeared to be a different person, and if that frightened him it was tough-titty. If she could control it she would. Or perhaps she wouldn't. Maybe, just maybe, she needed to do it from time to time, just to prove to herself that she still could.

This was the beginning of the end with her parents: they were all on a train going to Skegness. Jane was sitting beside her mother and her father was in the window seat facing them. They were travelling by train because her father had lost his licence and he said the journey was too far for her mother to drive. Nobody was sitting next to him (because he glowered when anybody came close) so he'd put his evening newspaper on the seat. Jane liked being with the two of them, especially in public. They were both very good-looking. And she didn't just think that because she was their child. People were always saying what a handsome couple they made. Her mother in her youth had been a beauty queen. Jane cherished the photo of her at Minehead with her hand on her right hip, walking around the swimming pool ('Like a tea pot' her father had sneered). In the back-ground of the picture four men in suits and ties sat behind a trestle table. They were all smoking cigarettes and one of them was writing on a score sheet with a fountain pen. Jane often looked at the photograph. After she'd studied her mother, she would always then look at the man with the pen. He had thick white hair and he looked like a mischie-vous wizard. Her mother said she could have made a career in the beauty business but her heart wasn't in it; anyway, when Jane's father came onto the scene, he told her he didn't want her parading around in a swimsuit. Not that he made a living respectably, but people trusted him when he sold them his clapped-out cars. He looked genuinely wounded if they questioned whether the mileage had been tampered with. Tom Hackett made a good con man. He had an honest face.

His mother called her father Hackett. Never Tom. It seemed appropriate to the distance they maintained between themselves.

Night had fallen and Jane, bored by the long train journey, had opened her mother's shiny handbag and her mother had gone mad. There was no warning before she slapped Jane on the side of her head and shouted that the bag was her private property and Jane had no right to look in it. Jane's head had spun. The white bulbs in the carriage roof went around and around. When, many years later, she recounted the incident to the old psychiatrist she said she had been frightened she was going to puke up in the carriage. She remembered that her father had stood up for her but her mother had then turned on him. She said that Jane never went into his wallet – did she? Because that was private. He said that he wouldn't have cared if she did. But it was always about privacy with her mother, she had so little to call her own. Oh, there were plenty of dresses and things, but just not enough feelings that she hadn't got from other people.

'From other people? Feelings? Explain that to me,' the psychiatrist once asked Jane.

'She woke up each day and I never knew how she was going to be.'

'That must have been hard.'

Oh, fuck off, she thought. Fuck off with always pretending to be sympathetic. I'll tell you without you doing all that psycho-psycho stuff.

'What do you think?' she had said to him. 'How would you feel?'

'Well . . . I think I would have felt . . . afraid.'

'Scared to bits every morning. The post comes, right? She gets angry because my father has had a letter – and she doesn't recognize the writing so she thinks it's from a woman. And I can see her taking it into the kitchen and standing by the kettle and thinking of steaming it open. But she doesn't and now she feels guilty; she's angry with herself because she hates herself for feeling like this. And that makes her worse because she . . . then she gets angry with me . . .'

'Go on.'

'. . . I was only looking at her. I only wanted to help. She was my mum. You know? She was my mum and I was just a child. Four? Five? I don't know. But I already knew about her. I knew everything she was feeling. It was like . . . I was a part of her and I . . . if she'd picked me up and held me I could have helped her. But she never did.'

'So you wanted to be held by her?'

'I didn't say that. I said I could have helped her.'

'Tell me about how that made you feel.'

'Mind your own business.'

'Do you find it difficult to tell me?'

'I don't want you to talk to me like she did.'

'Is that what I'm doing?'

'I just said so, didn't I?'

23

'Then how would you like me to talk to you?'

'Just once I'd like somebody to talk to me like I was a person and not some . . . somebody who can't cope.'

Afterwards she thought this: good things, good feelings, even bad feelings inside you, are all right so long as they're hatched by you. If everything you feel is borrowed from somebody else then you're in big trouble.

She looks towards the bed again and says 'Well?' before turning a full circle, showing off her clothes. She then puts the ravioli in the brown paper bag she got from the book-shop, anchors the wine under her arm and goes out of the flat.

3

Maude lives two doors along the corridor. Maria Callas can still be heard from inside her room as well as the voices of Alf and Maude raised in laughter. Jane is trying to hold a smile on her face despite her anxiety at having to face two people in a confined space. Her cheek muscles are now so taut that she's not sure what she looks like as she knocks on Maude's door. The voices behind the door cease. Jane waits. Now the music goes silent. The door remains unanswered. Jane knocks again. The silence inside continues. She understands. She walks back to her flat, her head a little bowed. Just as she reaches her door she hears a peal of laughter from Maude's flat.

Downstairs, the front door bangs open. Jane looks down the stairwell and sees a man in a blue overall dart into the long hallway. He has a scrap of paper and a mobile phone in his right hand, a blue metal tool box in his left and a sense of urgency about him. He is as lean as a fox from trying to fit too much into each day. Scenting Jane, he looks up at her and asks: 'Where's your boiler, love?'

'I'm sorry?'

'Your boiler?'

'Don't know. In the cellar?'

'Ta.'

Jane lets herself back into her flat. She shivers, puts her undelivered gifts onto the kitchen table, and then she opens the wine and pours herself a glass of the sour pink liquid. She takes a sip as she stares out of the window. A woman is at a kitchen sink in the building behind hers. The city buildings are close, separated by small back-to-back yards as deep and as dark as wells. While Jane watches the woman a man wearing a work-crumpled shirt comes up behind her. He puts his arm around her waist and leans his stubbly chin on her right shoulder. She reaches up to rub the back of his head. They kiss but Jane is not taken in by them. She can see the weariness and habit.

Returning to the cupboard she gets out another wine glass which she half fills with wine. She then takes both of the glasses out onto the landing where she pauses for a moment. Maria Callas is again audible from Maude's flat. She is tempted to go back and knock on the door but she doesn't have the energy for a confrontation. Instead, she goes downstairs, along the hallway corridor and pauses at the cellar door. Beyond it is a set of steep dark wooden steps. She peers into the darkness, and then she goes down.

The noise of the plumber is immediately audible from a room somewhere to the front of the cellar, which is full of the junk of former tenants. There are pools of water on the concrete floor; the ceiling is garlanded with cobwebs. The only light comes from a single, unshaded bulb.

She approaches the noise of the plumber, turns into a room blackened by coal-dust and there, in the tiny furnace of torchlight clasped under his armpit, she sees him working at the old boiler. The white metal cover is leaning against the damp wall.

Jane says: 'I thought you might like a drink.'

The plumber drops his torch – alarmed by the intrusion. It goes out.

'I'm sorry!'

'Don't panic. No harm done,' Jane hears as he scrabbles around in the darkness. 'Wait a moment.'

Jane hears the moist click of the rubber torch switch and then the beam is directed into her face. She recoils. The plumber apologizes and turns it away from her.

He can see that Jane is shaking so he approaches her carefully. He is a little older than she had thought when she first saw him: early forties, but with a good head of black hair, a sportsman's taut stride and a strong chin. He has a confident smile and there is something of the predator in him.

'You nearly gave me a heart attack,' he says, taking the

opportunity to pat his heart with his right palm. 'Feel it,' he suggests.

'I shouldn't have come down here.'

'Is that for me?'

Jane looks at the glass in her hand, remembers, and gives it to the man.

'I'm on call tonight so I probably shouldn't – still. . .' He takes a sip and grimaces. 'Blimey this is rough old stuff, isn't it?'

It doesn't taste rough to Jane. All the wine she has ever tried has tasted the same, except once, with *him*, when he took her out for a meal and made her sip the wine slowly.

'Well?' he had asked her gently.

'It's lovely,' Jane had said. And it was. But now she couldn't remember what lovely tasted like. She had been seventeen years old – it was almost a lifetime ago.

'I'm very cheap to take out,' she had told him, having heard the line delivered by a girl on television.

'You deserve to be loved properly,' he had replied, and at the time he had seemed to mean it.

He took her to a place that called itself a bistro. The menu was on a blackboard. There were seven small square tables with red-chequered cloths, a red candle in a wine bottle on each one and, on a small raised platform by the door, a girl in a long, woollen jumper playing a Spanish guitar. She sang her sad songs with a quiet determination, indifferent to the audience eating their reasonably-priced French food.

*

The plumber is taken aback by Jane's remoteness. He sees it as a challenge and he can't resist the challenge of a good-looking woman.

He says: 'Stay and watch a craftsman at work if you like . . . if you've got nothing better to do.'

'No. I haven't,' Jane admits and settles her shoulder against a blackened wall to watch him work. He puts the torch onto a ledge and directs the beam towards the job.

'I don't know when this was last serviced,' he says, adopting the tone he employs when he wants to frighten people into spending money. 'Your landlord's playing with fire. Literally. If something happened and he didn't have a certificate. Well . . . Still, I'm here now, aren't I?' He turns and beams a smile at her.

Jane is in bed, lying on her back. The man on top of her is no longer smiling, as he forces himself into her. She's unengaged in the act – although not resisting. He looks down at her immobile face and sees it as a challenge so he pushes harder. But soon he slumps and collapses onto her. She pushes him away and he rolls onto his back and she momentarily feels the cold absence of him. Immediately he is asleep.

Jane is sitting at the single kitchen chair when she hears the pipes begin to tick. She goes to the radiator and feels the bottom of it. Heat is bleeding in. She smiles. The plumber comes sheepishly to the door. He is buttoning his blue overall.

'I should be going,' he says. 'Fell asleep.'

'Yes.'

'I've. I mean. I've been working nights and days . . .'

'You're on call.'

'That's right. I'm on call.' He takes out his phone and checks for missed callers. There have been three. He will phone them all back and tell them he was mending a dodgy boiler in a cellar and he didn't hear it ring. He'll mention the filth down there because it's the detail that makes lies believable.

'Well . . .' he says, transferring his attention back to Jane. 'That was . . .' He tries a smile. It usually suffices when words don't but the woman he has just been with is not his normal type; she won't be satisfied with a boyish smile. She won't send him on his way with a slap on the arse like a fond mother, reassuring him that boys will be boys. He's found out too late that she's the sort who takes nothing lightly. But too many of them end up like that, whatever they seem like in the beginning.

'It doesn't matter,' Jane says.

'I don't do this. I mean, I don't want you to think . . .'

'I said it doesn't matter.'

'I've got two kiddies. It matters to me.'

He makes to go. Then he pauses and says: '. . . What if I called again? How would that be?'

'With the kiddies?' Jane thinks it's an innocent enough question but it provokes his anger.

'Don't be stupid.' He gets a grip of himself when he glimpses an awful scene from an alternative future: his two daughters playing on the rumpled sheets of the mad girl's bed.

'So why would you come?'

'I don't know. I wouldn't. I mean, I won't.'

'Because you love me? So much love that there is no more to be had?'

'I don't know about that.'

He leaves her after forcing a dry kiss onto her cold cheek.

Jane can't sleep so she strips the bed at 3 a.m. By eight o'clock she is in the launderette again. She opens her paper-back book and takes out the photograph which has a tiny hole in the centre where she pinned it to the wall. She glances at the photo and then slips it into the back of her book. As she reads, Alf comes in with a plastic bag of his washing. When he sees her it's apparent from his expression that his immediate instinct is flight, but because he knows he'll have to face her sooner or later, he decides to get it out of the way. Otherwise he'll be fretting about it all day.

'Fourteen years I've been in that place,' he announces, approaching Jane and standing over her. 'After the missus went. Fourteen years.'

He's already worked out how he's going to explain it all to her, but he knows with a woman (or girl, really, because that's how he sees her) like Jane, he'll have to take it slowly. So he lets this sink in as he opens a machine and pushes in his washing. At the bottom of his bag is a small box of washing powder. He tamps in a measure and then slides his pound coins into the slot. Taking the chair beside Jane's, he sighs to signal the exertion of stoking the machine. He sighs after most activities nowadays, however unstrenuous; a habit the elderly have when the world has begun to weary them. '. . . and that's the first time anybody's invited me in.'

'We were going to have a party,' Jane says.

'I know. I know . . .'

'I did knock.'

'Yeah.'

'But nobody came. And I'd used a ribbon on some wine, and I brought a tin like Maude said.'

'I'm sorry, love. You see, well, we'd had a few and then she opened the gin . . .'

'I came when she told me to come. I wasn't late.'

'No. Well you see, I got there a bit early and, well, you knocked, and she kind of looked at me and . . . See, the thing is, you don't get many opportunities at my age.'

'Did you have a nice time?'

'Yeah. I suppose we did.'

'Did you spend the night with her?'

'I'm not sure that's any of . . . no I didn't.'

'Why didn't you?'

'It didn't seem polite. Anyway, best to wake up alone when you get to my age if you get my drift.'

'No.'

'Nobody looks their best in the mornings when you get over forty.'

'It's nice having the heating on again, isn't it?'

'Yeah. Except if you want to know the truth, I don't really feel the cold.'

'I do.'

Alf looks at her.

'What?' Jane asks him.

'Nothing.'

'Tell me.'

'I can't figure it out. Lovely girl like you locked away in there. It doesn't seem right. I mean I've had my life. Used it all up. But you . . . how long've you been there now?'

'Did you love your wife?'

'Gawd, no.'

'Why did you marry?'

'Search me.'

'Have you ever loved anybody?'

He laughs and ruminates. 'Yeah.'

'Who was she?'

'I don't know. I only saw her once. When I was a young laddie. In a club. The Legion I think it was.'

'Tell me.'

'I saw this woman sitting on her own and I swear I fell right in love with her there and then. She had this light hair, cut like . . . well, you know, all that kind of underneath palaver and this . . . this look about her, I can't describe it . . .'

'Yes?'

'Well, I asked her if she wanted to dance. I'm not the most confident kind of bloke in that respect. But she said she'd like that. And I said well I'll be straight back, because I needed a – you know – I needed to use the lavatory. Anyhow, when I got back out she was gone. And I never saw her again. I went back there time and time again . . . And I think about her every day of my life. Honest I do. Every day of my life. Is that love?'

'Yes. That's love. Of a sort.'

Alf takes out his newspaper which is rolled up in the side pocket of his large grey mac, and unrolls it. 'Anyway, you get back to your book,' he says. 'I didn't come in here to disturb you.'

Distracted, Jane re-opens her book, but before she finds her place in it Alf shakes out his newspaper and reads the headline on the front page. Jane glances across at it. It's a local paper. Under the blaring headline is a photograph of a man whose body has been found in a park. The photo is that of the man on Jane's bookmark.

Jane tears her eyes away and looks back towards the washing in the dryer but she can't contain herself. Her eyes slide back to the newspaper and stay there until she forces them down towards her book and the small edge of the photo which protrudes from the top. Unaware of all this, the old man continues to read. Jane slips out the photo. She looks at it, then across at the paper.

4

The story of 'the body in the park' is advertised in royal blue ink on the hoarding outside the newsagent's. Jane is standing beside it, reading the front page of the newspaper she has just bought. People push past her as she hungrily scans the text: JohnEvans/35/apianotunerandmusician/Localpark/Foxesdisturbedthebody/noapparentmotive/missingfortwodays.

How did they know it was foxes? Jane wonders and realizes she must have wondered it out loud because a woman in a business suit pauses as she passes her. She then walks on, irritated because she had thought Jane was asking directions of her. One night, when she used to live in a nicer neighbourhood, Jane saw a fox in the middle of a school field. At first she thought it was a cat because it was sitting calmly, watching her. When she walked along the iron railing fence it stood up and followed her. Each time she stopped, it stopped and sat down again. She wanted to go and stroke it but she remembered somebody telling her that foxes were dangerous creatures, like squirrels. They looked beautiful but they'd bite you if they got the chance and then you'd end up in A & E waiting for four hours for some tired, young, foreign doctor to come and attend to you behind your curtain.

This is what she can't fathom: why she just can't seem to concentrate any more. What was it? Foxes. And how did she get there? Because they had found his body in the park. And now she feels it, like a flush of blood. No. Not blood. Like the feeling of the epidural going into her spine. Electric and cold and then everything around it going numb.

It didn't matter to her they had to cut her to get Billy out. The lights were so bright in that room in the high-rise tower and the window was tall and wide and she could see right across the city. She loved it in there: the way the nurses seemed to be interested in her and adored Billy. They called her 'poppet' and bitched about the other mothers to her: somehow she was the chosen one. She supposed it was because she was young and she didn't make a fuss about the pain of the stitches and Billy took to the breast straight away. She would have faced any pain for her baby. She still would.

When Jane returns to the launderette Alf is minding her washing. He has not taken off his coat (he doesn't do that in public nowadays), but he has rolled up his sleeves. He's not the kind who would stare at the machine for hours on end, lost in his thoughts. No, Jane sees him as a very practical type. Once he told her how he'd built a porch on his house and he hadn't had any training in it. He'd constructed the walls out of breeze blocks, plastered them, put a roof on and tiled the floor and it was still there today. He'd offered to take her to see it and when she'd laughed he'd laughed too and that almost made her want to go with him – on the bus, to see his bloody porch. But watching Alf, wondering what he was thinking, Jane wished that just once she could get right inside somebody else's head. She'd know then whether she was mad or not.

Alf sees her paper and says 'You could have had a butcher's at mine.'

'I wanted one for myself.'

'There's nothing in it. Still, I don't know what I expect to find in it – never has been anything in the local papers except yesterday's news and people complaining about the bus service and the rates.'

When Jane sits down next to him, he says 'Oh, your whatsit's finished.' Alf has taken her sheets out of the dryer and folded them neatly into a pile on the waist-high wooden shelf. On top of the pile is a pair of her nice blue lace knickers, also folded, and the presence of them there embarrasses him. She put them on for Maude's party and the plumber took them off for her. She felt his fast, hot breath on her breasts as he looked down at her body. He wanted her to undo his overalls but it took ages because there were so

37

many metal buttons. It surprised her as he stepped out of them that he smelled so fresh. She'd expected him to smell of sweat and metal pipes.

Jane puts the knickers into her bag. She holds the warm sheets up to her cheek, and then puts them in too. The old man watches her. It feels indecent to him, seeing her doing all this, almost as if he'd seen her naked.

It's raining when Jane goes back outside. The rain brings to her mind the photo and the man in the paper. How she could have forgotten it all she doesn't quite know. This is what the drugs do to her: they close up the space in her head so she can't feel the big things explode. Before, when she was cross, she knew how to be cross. People didn't like it but that was tough-titty because she was never cross without a reason. Now she doesn't get cross, just confused. When she stopped taking the tablets she got properly cross again but then they came to fetch her and put her back on the ward.

Jane feels the rain go down the back of her neck as she stands at the door of the second-hand bookshop looking in – but it's closed because it's Wednesday and it looks very desolate in the rain. She thinks there's nothing sadder than an old shop with the lights off. It reminds her of the Christmas Days she has spent walking around on her own looking for somewhere to go. She has never been that bothered about company, but she does like places where she can be around people without having to talk to them. That's why she washes her bedclothes so often. Once she joined a gym because she had seen one in a television drama and liked the idea of sitting on the cycling machine with other people around her. The gym was in the basement of an old college and it cost her £27 to join, (which she couldn't really afford – but she went without some meals) and £12.50 a month. When she went for her induction the athletic young girl with the tracksuit and clipboard who showed her around didn't explain things properly and Jane found herself sitting on the cycle and trying to pedal but it was too hard and her legs hurt. She already felt stupid because the other women in there had the right clothes on and all she had was her old swimming costume and some dark tights. The girl came up to ask her why she was crying but she couldn't stop so they took her into the office and called for the police. The police told her she was being a nuisance and she should get her clothes and go home (actually, he said 'Piss off home', in a whisper). One of the policemen fancied the gym girl, Jane could tell. It made him more officious than he needed to be with her. When he took her arm to make her go back to the changing room, his fingers left a bruise. Walking home, the police drove past her. The officious one was laughing and Jane knew he was laughing about her. He was eating a Cornish pasty from a cellophane wrapper. Jane only needed people when other people hurt her. But soon the feelings went away because the tablets packed them down into the tight ball in her stomach.

When she returned to the gym the following week to ask

for her £27 back they wouldn't give it to her because they said the joining fee wasn't refundable.

All this comes to her as Jane looks up at the tall façade of the bookshop while the grey raindrops fall towards her face in slow motion.

Jane is in her flat. She is standing by the window looking out at the rain. She paces the small space of her cell. The newspaper is on the kitchen table, the photograph beside it. She keeps returning to it. Some decision has to be made – but she's confused.

She goes out of her flat and along the corridor – past Maude's room and pauses at another door. She knocks. There is a pause. A bolt is drawn back, then another, a lock is sprung and the door opens to reveal Alf. He wears a suspicious expression Jane has never seen on his face before. She wouldn't like to get on the wrong side of Alf, that's for sure. Seeing who has knocked, he relaxes, but not entirely. He doesn't like unexpected visitors. People always bring obligations with them, and he's glad to have been free of them since his wife died.

'It wasn't her,' Jane says.

'I'm not with you,' Alf says, still holding on to the door handle.

'The woman in the club. You didn't fall in love with her. You fell in love with who you wanted her to be.'

'Well, I don't know about that.'

'If you'd danced with her and she hadn't disappeared

you'd have found out just how ordinary she was. And then you wouldn't . . . Do you see?'

'You could leave me my memories, you know. I mean if you'd be so kind. Because that's what you're left with when you get to my age.'

'Otherwise people get confused about what real love is – you need two people for real love.'

Alf shuts the door slowly. Jane realizes immediately what she has done. She goes to knock but stops herself. On her way back to her flat she pauses outside Maude's room. Beside her door is a radiator. Jane looks at it and in looking at it makes a decision which leads her downstairs to the cellar door. Opening it, she goes down the dark stairs. Ahead of her is the small room where the boiler is housed. But it is too dark and menacing to go in.

Back in her flat she rummages in her drawer. She calls out: 'Where did you put the torch?' But then she remembers the story in the newspaper. He is gone.

She goes into the kitchen, opens a drawer and takes out a short stub of candle.

'You never put anything back where you get it from, do you?' she calls, because already she has forgotten.

When she goes out into the corridor again, Alf is leaving the house carrying a leather bag of empty stout bottles. The bottles clink together with the rhythm of his walk. Jane can't meet his eye but follows him downstairs, and when the front door is shut behind him she returns to the cellar. Once inside she lights the candle, shields it with her palm and approaches the boiler. She peers in at the blue pilot flame which is behind a small glass door. She slides the door open and tries to blow out the flame but she can't. Next to the boiler is a switch. She switches it off. The flame goes out.

5

A boy sits in the half-light of his bedroom. His eyes are glued to a television screen on which a red Ferrari Enzo is tearing around the deserted early morning streets of New York City. The black controller cradled between his palms is linked umbilically to his games console. His thumbs massage the buttons and tiny joystick. His reflexes are sharpened by the rod of tension between his shoulder blades. In a clock at the top right-hand corner of the screen the seconds tick down. The Ferrari is chasing the ghost shadow of its best lap time. The finishing line is in sight. When the car crosses it the boy brakes hard, sending the vehicle slewing around in a cloud of tyre-smoke. The ghost car recedes into the distance. The boy lays the controller down onto the bed beside him and reaches for a wine gum from the bag split open on his knee.

'William,' a woman's voice calls. 'Five minutes.'

William blinks. A moment passes.

'Did you hear me?'

'Yes,' the boy says as if he is afraid of breaking the silence in the room. His voice barely carries to the door.

'William?'

'Yes?'

'Five minutes.'

He picks up the games controller again and weighs it in his hands. His thumbs flex in tiny motions. The screen is taunting him. From the small speaker of the TV, rock music plays. He toggles the joystick, accepts the first option he is presented with, and the game counts him down. But when the claxon sounds and the gantry lights show green his car remains idling on the start line. The boy throws down the controller which bounces on the mattress. He goes to the door of his bedroom which is slightly ajar. He waits in the slit of illumination from the landing. He is comfortable here, in his own ray of light. An old memory warms him. He is eleven years old but already he is beginning to wonder if he feels the same as the other children he knows. He suspects he may not because his life is riddled with anxieties so acute that when they surface they rob him of his hunger.

The boy feels a pressure on the door and it opens a little. He looks down at the wet nose of the black Labrador. Guiltily she looks up at him, imploring him not to tell with an age-old sadness. He reaches down and feels the soft pelt of fur beneath her chin. Her tail wags but the expression on her face does not change. He kneels and she licks his face.

'William?' he hears.

'Yes.'

'William?'

'What?'

'Have you got the dog up there?'

'No,' he lies.

'Have you washed your hands?'

'Yes,' he lies.

'Two minutes.'

The boy slides his back down the door jamb and sinks to the floor. The dog rests her chin on his thigh. She waits for a moment before looking into his face to judge whether he is happy to let her remain there. He is.

6

Jane opens the door of her flat to Maude.

'It's gone again,' Maude says.

'Yes, I was just going to call them,' Jane tells her.

'Would you mind doing that? Only it's becoming quite a trial, isn't it?' Maude tries to peer beyond Jane into her flat. She won't angle for an invitation until she has judged the state of it.

'No more credit on your electric card?'

'Not much. I used most of it up last night.' Being a woman, she doesn't feel the need to explain herself to Jane. So far as she is concerned, her generation was the last to have ordered their priorities correctly, and hers would always remain to find a man. She'd never quite understood the young girls she saw going out dancing with other young girls. Some of them even had husbands and boyfriends at home.

Alf emerges from his flat. He has faced Jane, now he has to offer Maude an altogether different apology. He had heard her talking out in the corridor and knew it would be easier if she was in company when he did it.

He chooses to continue the attack on Jane, despite having already forgiven her for what she had said to him. 'Only memories are what keep you warm at night. Know what I mean?' he says, but Jane ignores him.

'The boiler's out again,' Maude announces.

'I know it is.'

'And this young lady has kindly volunteered to go and call out the plumber again.'

'Has she now?' Alf says. What's her game now? he wonders. Mad as a bloody fruitcake. Now she's talking as if she's never met the girl before – all this 'young lady' palaver. Still, best to go along with it.

'Well I can't leave the house. Not with my leg the way it is.'

Alf looks down at Maude's legs. They'd seemed all right last night. He didn't remember her complaining when she patted the bed beside her and guided his hand inside her gown and he felt the softness of her breast. It gave him quite a start, that did. He'd quite forgotten how soft a woman could feel.

'Shouldn't either of you be walking round here at night on your own. Bad leg or no bad leg. I'll go.'

'Well, one of you should.' Maude is disappointed because she had been hoping that Alf would come in to her flat so they could try again. The next time she was sure they'd manage it more elegantly.

'I'll come with you,' Jane says.

'Is there any need for that?' Maude asks Alf, jealousy springing up from a well she had thought was dry. The fierceness of it shocks her. She'd lost one man because of her jealous rages, but they had served her well and fear of them had kept her two husbands on the straight and narrow.

'No, I'd like to,' Jane says.

'I don't mind the company,' Alf tells Maude.

Jane goes to fetch her coat from the flat. When she has gone, Maude gives Alf a look that chills him. He knows he should run while he still has the chance, but then Maude opens her coat and she is not wearing anything underneath and she still looks like a woman and he knows he is lost.

Jane collects her mac from behind her door and follows Alf down the stairs. Outside, facing the chill, she wants to link her arm in his, but is afraid he won't like it so she resists the impulse.

'...The fact is you're right,' Alf says. 'Fact is I know exactly what you're saying ... but there's always a chance isn't there that she might have been different? And neither you or me could ever know that for sure.' The time he spent with Maude now feels tainted; second-best.

The traffic speeds by on the main road, the tyres swish in the rain. The yellow of the streetlights is pooled like liquid gold on the glossed tarmac. The couple shamble towards the phone booth separated by two feet of cold pavement.

Jane is sitting on her bed. She has been waiting for two hours for the plumber to arrive. The photo bookmark is pinned back in position above her bed. She has dressed herself up and had a bath. But she is now cold, her breath again visible in the air. When she hears the front door open on the ground floor she springs up, goes into the corridor and catches sight of the shape of a man going through the cellar door. He is carrying a blue metal box of tools.

Jane waits for a moment then follows him down. As she descends the cellar stairs she can hear the man whistling; a bastard form of music-making which has always irritated her. Her father used to do it when he was feeling cocksure, hands deep in his pockets, playing with his balls. He'd whistle in the bathroom in the morning because he liked the way it echoed against the tiles and she'd follow him in there to the smell of shit and Old Spice.

When Jane approaches the boiler room and sees the back of the man immediately she knows it's not the plumber who came the night before. She starts when she disturbs something metal on the floor and looks down to see that it is a rusty shelf-bracket.

'Was it you that called?' He's a gone-to-seed-early fifty-year-old. No chin, thin hair, sagging stomach barely contained by his tartan shirt, a wisp of belly hair peeping out of the gap between the straining buttons. But the look he gives her suggests he still thinks he's got what it takes.

'No. It was somebody else,' Jane says.

'Somebody's been playing soppy monkeys.'

'What?'

'This was working last night, right?' He turns to the boiler like a barrister.

'Yes. We had heating after the other man came.'

'Yeah, well somebody's switched the juice off.' He flicks a switch and says 'Job done,' watching for Jane's reaction.

'Where is he?' Jane asks.

'Who?'

'The man from last night.'

'Oh, right. I get it.' The man says, a smile slowly dawning.

'I don't think you do.'

'He's probably at home in his nice warm house with his nice warm missus, if I know Ian.'

'Ian?'

'That's right. Didn't he give you his name? . . . You missing him already are you?' He laughs and Jane backs out of the room.

Jane is in bed. The lights are out and she can see coloured clouds in the dark: purples and greys swirl against the black. She has slept for fifteen minutes and woken having had a dream she can't quite remember. Since the hospital, since the loss of Billy, she has slept in chapters. Each hour she has woken from another hellish instalment only to tumble again into a dark hole in the company of new taunting demons. Hearing a knock on the door, she waits. After another knock she gets out of bed and goes to the door. She is sticky from the warmth of the covers.

'He said you were disappointed it wasn't me.'

It's the plumber from the night before: Ian. He is wearing a black Levi's jacket, a white shirt and combat trousers and he is carrying a cellophane bunch of petrol-station carnations. His hair is still wet from the shower. 'Street door was on the latch. I came straight up.'

Jane takes his hand and draws him into the flat.

'I knew,' he says. 'Last night I told you there was something between us . . . Christ, you're keen aren't you?'

Jane is undressing him in the dim light of the room.

'Be quiet,' she orders.

This time, on the bed, Jane is in charge. She sits above the man, arches her back and sighs just as the man does. She slumps down and buries her face in his shoulder. He strokes the wet hair on the nape of her neck as she lies on him. Reaching around her, he pulls up the quilt to cloak her shoulders.

He sleeps with his back towards her. She whispers: 'We missed all this, didn't we? All this time we could have had together. All these nights. Even here in this terrible, terrible place . . . except you would have made it all right. I know you would . . . What happened? What happened to you?'

Ian the plumber rolls over to face her. Groggily, he says, 'What?' Sleep has made him ugly and his breath stale.

'Nothing.'

'I thought you said something.'

'No.'

'Yes you did. What did you say?'

'I was talking to somebody else.'

'Who?'

'Somebody.'

'You're bloody weird – you know that?' He sits up and yawns. '. . . I've got to go.' He doesn't want her now that he's had her. It's always like that with him and women. The tenderness he feels for them burns off along with the lust and afterwards he just wants to be left alone. Sometimes he despises them because they've seen the weakness in him. Like his mother said, men always show their weakness in bed while women show their strength.

'Why do you have to go?'

'You know why.' His body is milky white. She reaches up and touches a birthmark on his right shoulder. She wants to feel the temperature of his skin but he misinterprets it as a gesture of apology. He turns and lowers his face to hers. When he kisses her she feels afraid of him.

'You're a strange one,' he says.

'I'm not.'

'Yes you are.'

'Why do you say that?'

He laughs and turns away from her again to put on his

shirt. Then he rummages under the bed for his trousers, stands and tugs them up. Like most men, Jane thinks, he looks better with his clothes on.

'Don't do that with the boiler again. I don't like other people knowing my business.' Clothed, he's back in charge; there's a spring in his step, he's cock of the walk.

'What other people?'

'Pete. The one who came round here earlier. He's got a big mouth.'

'Pete?'

'You can call me on the mobile – but don't go off on one if I'm at home and I can't talk.'

'Go off on one?'

'Get narked.'

'All right.'

'And if she picks it up don't say anything.'

'Nothing?'

'Just say I gave you the number for emergencies. Tell her I said you could call if something happened to the boiler overnight – and something's happened and you're worried.'

'All right.'

'Oh yeah. And say you're sorry for disturbing her. She likes people being polite to her.'

'Would she be polite to me?'

'What do you think?'

'What's her name?'

'Donna.'

'I don't know anybody called Donna.'

'Well let's keep it that way shall we.'

Jane is afraid that something she's done has offended him. Perhaps she has not been the kind of woman he wanted her to be.

Jane, in her dressing gown, is sitting at the kitchen table reading the newspaper when Ian the plumber comes in from the lavatory.

'So . . .' He wants to negotiate, Jane can tell. He doesn't know if this is the end or the beginning of something.

Jane turns the paper around so that he can see it. She remembers now why she wanted him to come: she needed a witness so that somebody else would hold the memory of how she acted on the day she learned he was dead. But what would the plumber remember of today? Half an hour in the bedroom and the cost of a bunch of carnations. Somehow she has to make it count; she needs to focus. What does she feel? She strains but the emotions are out of reach.

'What?' he says.

'Did you see this in the paper?'

'Yeah.'

'And?'

'What do you mean – and?'

'Don't you care?'

'Care? I never knew him, love, so why should I care?'

'He died. People should care.'

'Well, all right, I care. How's that?'

Ian the plumber waits for a signal that they are going to

discuss what they will do next but the woman at the table continues to stare at the newspaper. She is good-looking, no doubt about that. If only she was more normal he could see himself making a habit of coming around here on a regular basis. That would suit him down to the ground. And the flat is clean, even by his high standards. He likes a woman who keeps herself neat and tidy, inside and out.

'Well do they say how he died?' he tries.

'He was hit on the head.'

'With a blunt object?'

'How do you know?'

'I don't.' He laughs. 'That's what they always say isn't it? "Hit over the head with a blunt object".'

'She did it.'

'Who did it?'

'She did.'

'Right.' Ian the plumber is anxious now to get away. Jane decides to let him go.

Bonkers, Ian the plumber tells himself as he skips down the stairs, whistling. He seems to have got away scot-free so that's a result. But already he regrets giving the girl his mobile number. It will be the first thing that comes to his mind when he wakes, anxious, in the dead of night and he will curse himself for his stupidity.

7

It had been suggested to Don and Fiona that the boy in their care would benefit from owning a dog. Since William's arrival ('on approval', Fiona told her friend – they were fostering him with a view to adoption), he had disappointed them, particularly Fiona, in that he had never been an affectionate child. It was only when she realized this that she understood why it was she had wanted to become a parent: she needed love to be demonstrated to her in a way her husband seemed incapable of. But the thin, intense boy, who had taken up residence in their second bedroom, had shrunk away at the prospect of any contact. He had been unfailingly polite, for which Fiona had been grateful in the beginning – she had been afraid she would not be able to take him out with her – but she had recently begun to question Don whether he thought it was wrong for her to feel as though she hated the child. Don refused to countenance the suggestion but had called in the support worker who had sat down with them one evening and, almost without them noticing, had interrogated them for nearly two hours about how William was settling in. Almost as soon as the woman had arrived Fiona had wanted a gin. Her thirst for it became so strong that soon all she could think about was the promise of the chill of the glass against her palms, the soft fizz of the tonic teasing the half slice of fresh lemon, the cube of ice cold against her lips as she drank. When she could bear it no longer she had gone to the kitchen under the pretence of making a cup of tea. While she was in there she could hear the boy in his bedroom playing on his X-Box. She strained to hear what Don was saying to the woman, hoping – that with her out of the room – he would confide the truth. But Don had never been one for her version of the truth and had used her absence as an opportunity to reassure the visitor that his wife was just going through a bad patch and she adored the boy really.

William had been summoned to sit between Don and Fiona on the settee and tell them all how he was feeling. It was, however, immediately evident that he found it hard to put his feelings into words.

'That's just boys for you,' Don said, the trace of his Southport accent grating on Fiona in the way it tended to do when she was tired. She found it ugly and said it made him sound stupid which he clearly wasn't. But she had never managed to train him out of it.

'Boys, eh, William?' Don smiled and William had not known what he was supposed to say to that. But he had been repulsed by Don's heavy hand ruffling the hair at the nape of his neck. It was, as far as he could remember, the first time he had touched him. Sometimes he felt that Don was afraid he might break him if there was any physical contact between them. On the other hand, the woman he was supposed to call 'Mum' was always trying to make him kiss her and hold her, and stand up in the bath so she could wrap a warm towel around him. He hated that more than anything else.

'How would you feel about showing me your room?' the visitor had said to William, and neither Don nor Fiona could take offence at the suggestion, even though the intent was naked enough.

'Take her upstairs and show her your room, William,' Don had instructed before William had had a chance to stand up and comply. Don had asked him what colour he had wanted to paint his room and made a big fuss about inviting him to B & Q to buy the paint (a 'blokes' outing'). But the red he had chosen wasn't quite to Don's taste, so they had bought five litres of a sober blue, which William had allowed himself to seem convinced was a better shade for a bedroom. And then Don had made another big show of inviting William to help him paint the room – 'Just us men together, eh?' – and William had tried to do it properly and neatly but he kept getting specks of paint on the skirting boards. When Don had come over to him for the fourth time, taken his small brush and patiently gone over the area he had just painted, he didn't bother taking the brush back when Don offered it. Instead, he went to sit on the bed and watch Don at work. William's inclination had been to paint the wall in small squares, which he would then join up before the paint dried. Don's technique was physical and extrovert, huge swathes of wall covered with every sweep of the brush. When they were finished the blue walls made William feel cold and sad.

The man he was encouraged to call 'Dad' was a large character who everybody in the street seemed to like because he was jovial. He would help anybody out, in fact Fiona once accused him of waiting at the window for the sole purpose of offering a helping hand: he watched for cars needing to be bump-started; he eyed the leaves floating into the gutters so that, when they were full, he could fetch his aluminium ladder and clean them out; he looked out for seized locks to be oiled, washers to be replaced, packages to be taken in. He had a garage full of tools, all stored against their painted silhouettes on his huge white-board. He had jars full of pristine screws, two workmates and an armoury of power tools. 'Weapons of mass construction' he called them; a joke he repeated to everyone he knew. He was a man who also had the practical gift of happiness but who just couldn't fathom the introverted boy who had arrived in his house. Having little interior life of his own he couldn't work out what William spent his time thinking about.

William had wanted to talk to the visitor alone because

she seemed kind and more interested in him than his new mother. She was also a tie to his old life, and that was important to him. So he had stood up at Don's instruction and the woman had stood up too, and smiled at Don and Fiona in a way that seemed to applaud their part in nurturing a child so well that he was now capable of standing without assistance. Her smile was broad enough not to alienate William, because by now she had become sufficiently concerned to wonder whether she should be considering taking the initial steps for his removal.

'Lead the way, William,' the woman had said, and the boy had been disappointed in her. After all, she knew his name was Billy, not William, but she had chosen not to use it. Perhaps he was expecting too much from her.

He had climbed the stairs quickly. He had a dislike of people standing too close behind him, even those he knew he should trust. So when the woman did arrive at his door and wait to be invited in, he was already sitting on the bed, his games controller in his hand. He was switching the game off because he thought it would be polite, but the woman didn't seem to mind.

He had shuffled up the bed to give her room to sit beside him; instead she went to the window and looked out at the street.

'. . . Do you play out much?' she had asked him, trying to make it sound as though the question had been prompted by her seeing a boy on his mountain bike riding under the streetlights.

'No.'

'Not much or not ever?'

'Not much,' he had lied, but he realized he couldn't lie to her because she had X-ray eyes and could see into his head. When she smiled and screwed up her eyes, the X-ray vision came into operation.

'Do you mind if I sit down?' she had asked him, and he was glad about that, in fact it almost made him like her again. She hadn't needed to ask his permission: she was a grown-up and grown-ups could do whatever they liked, but she had wanted to, because . . . because she saw him as a proper person with proper feelings.

'Tell me about your new school,' she had said, but he had shrugged and she knew she would have to refine the line of enquiry.

'Who's your class teacher?'

'Mr Long.'

'Is he nice?'

'He's a bit lairy.'

The woman's perfume was nice and soft and made Billy want to sit closer to her.

'Lairy?'

'He shouts at the boys.'

'Not at the girls?'

'No. He shouts at some of them.'

'And are the boys naughtier than the girls?'

'No. He's sexist.'

And from school they had gone on to talk about his

61

friends, or lack of them, and what he did after school – not much – and finally how he felt about his new home. But he didn't feel he could answer the question in a way that would be entirely truthful, because the truth was that he didn't exactly know how he felt.

'It's all right,' he had admitted.

'Is that good-all right or bad-all right?'

'Don't know.'

He had been aware at that moment of the tone of the woman's voice changing.

'Well what about . . . what about the food. Do you like what your mum cooks you?'

'She's not my mum.'

'All right. I'm sorry.' But the woman had got the answer she had been looking for. 'Well what about Don?'

'He doesn't do any cooking.'

'What does he do?'

'He goes to work before I go to school and he comes back at 6.35.'

'And when he comes back?'

'Don't know. He has his tea . . . He's good at making things.'

'Yes?'

'He made that,' William had said and pointed to the cabinet the games console was on.

'And did you help him?'

'No.'

'Did you want to help him?'

'I'm no good at woodwork.'

'But Don could have shown you how to do it.'

'I painted with him.'

'Yes? Tell me what you painted.'

'I painted that, over there.'

'Show me.'

William had got down from the bed, crossed the room and pointed to the area of wall beside the plug socket.

'It's very neat,' the woman had said.

'He went over it to make it right.'

'William . . .?'

'What?'

'Can you tell me . . . I know this is hard for you, but can you tell me how you feel living here?'

'It's all right.'

'I'm sorry. I know this is hard for you.'

'It's not hard,' William had said and went to his drawers, which he opened and took out a bar of Galaxy. He broke off two pieces, put the chocolate back in the drawer, returned to the bed and offered one of the pieces to the woman on his opened palm. Already it was melting.

'Are you sure?' she had said.

'Yes.'

'Thank you, Billy.'

Billy smiled. They chewed the chocolate in silence. It melted in their mouths until it became a fresh, liquid mush and then, too quickly, a sour, cloying tang to their saliva.

After a long silence the woman said, 'Would you say you were happy here?'

'Don't know.'

'All right, let me put it another way. Would you say you were unhappy?'

'No. Sometimes.'

'And what makes you . . .'

'Will you come?' Billy cut in.

'Where?'

'When I see my mum.'

'Yes. Well, I'll come or someone else will come.'

'I know, but will you come?'

'I'll try. I'm not sure it's all entirely been arranged yet.'

'It's on my calendar.'

'They've given you a date?'

'It's three months. Since last time. I wrote it down.'

'Yes, I think that's an approximate. . .'

'An hour and a half. That's what we get.'

'Yes I . . .'

'She'll be expecting to see me.'

'And that's important to you?'

When the woman left, she was concerned for the family, but no longer unduly concerned for the child. He had wisdom and a strength that had been gifted to him long before he'd arrived at Don and Fiona's.

8

Jane approaches the bookshop door. The rain continues to fall. When she goes in the bell is triggered. Patrick is drinking coffee from his usual mug at the counter. His hands are shaking.

'I've got the most shocking hangover,' he tells her. 'You know sometimes you wake up and you think you've got away with it. Then you get out of bed and you go – steady on, got to take it easy here. You get all that . . . stuff in your mouth. Does that happen to you?'

'No.'

'I didn't intend to get pissed. You don't – do you? But it creeps up on you in those evil clubs. I mean it's less that you make a decision to drink too much, more that you lose your appetite for sobriety.'

'Is it?'

'. . . Anyway, I'm debating whether to make myself sick. I can't stand puking but sometimes it helps doesn't it?'

'I've never tried.'

'Never? The old two fingers down the throat? I recommend it, but only under exceptional circumstances.'

While Jane considers what such circumstances might be, the door opens and a young man pops his head around: 'You buying?' he calls to Patrick.

'Well that depends on what you're selling today, Trevor. If you'd like to pop them down here, I'll have a look. Reminds me of that joke about the doctor – what was it? Pop your clothes down over there – on top of mine. Was that it?'

'Don't know, mate,' Trevor says, entering the shop in his fish-tailed parka, a tight, woollen hat compressing his brow over his wary eyes. Two heavy carrier bags of hardback books dangle from his arms. He hoists them onto the counter and massages the feeling back into his blood-drained fingers.

'I'm terrible with jokes,' Patrick says as he removes the new books from the bags and constructs two neat towers of them. 'You know I really envy people who can remember them. I'm absolutely hopeless. There was a sketch I saw the other night on late-night TV – what was it?'

Jane watches him with irritation. She wants Patrick to herself but he is taking his time with the books Trevor has brought in to sell him.

'. . . Two, three, five, seven, eight-fifty, ten, eleven, thirteen, fifteen, seventeen pounds-fifty pence for those,' Patrick says, then runs his finger down the second pile he has made and tallies it up as fifteen pounds. 'Thirty-two pounds and fifty pence, Trevor. That's the best I can do.'

'I'll take it.' Trevor snatches the money when Patrick holds it out towards him and dashes from the shop. Patrick watches him leave the premises. When he turns back towards Jane he sees her going away up the stairs. Switching his attention to the CCTV he watches her cross the monochrome room and sit on the wide shelf of the window recess. At this point a woman comes into the shop, and Patrick launches a neutered smile.

'Don't tell me,' Patrick says, 'book group.'

'How did you guess?'

'And what is this month's novel for consideration?'

When the woman has left, empty-handed, and Patrick has devoted ten minutes to watching an attractive young addict haunting the biographies section, he returns his attention to the CCTV monitor and sees that Jane has not moved from her perch at the window. He leaves his position at the counter and climbs the stairs. At the doorway at the top he waits. He doesn't want to crowd her. The room smells of mildew and it reminds him that there will be a point in the near future when he will have to address the condition of the building. This will necessitate a confrontation with Fergal, which Patrick will lose. The only outcome he can foresee is that the shop will close down and he will attempt to salvage some of the money he spent on the lease. His life will thus change – a prospect which terrifies rather than thrills him. If he had the courage he would blow his money on travelling, but he has never had much of that and so he'll look around for another low-risk, low-return venture to see him through the next unremarkable decade.

'Are you OK?' he says. '. . . Jane?' And finally she looks towards him but she still doesn't answer so he asks, 'Has something happened?'

'I expect.'

'No need to keep secrets from Uncle Patrick.'

'It's not a secret.'

'Is it not?'

'No.'

'So if it's not a secret, why don't you tell me?'

'I can't.'

'I've never let you down, have I Jane?'

Jane stands, pushes past Patrick and goes to the stairs. It has taken too long for him to come to her. She had everything ordered in her head: exactly what she would tell him, just how she would couch her request for his advice. She knew how careful she had to be to sound normal; any wrong note in her voice, anything approaching madness, would make him suspicious and push him away from her. But now she can't remember how she was going to do it.

Patrick follows her downstairs. Halfway down she stops and picks up a book from one of the treads.

'Say I bought a book from you,' she says. 'This one.'

'Three pounds.'

'Say I wanted to know who'd bought it in – could you tell me?'

'I doubt it. I mean I've got punters coming in all the time with bags of scabby paperbacks – cars full of old Uncle Fred's military books, house clearances, book reviewers, shoplifters like Trevor, all sorts of stuff all the time. I should say the answer was no.'

Jane puts the book back on the stairs.

'Why?' Patrick asks her.

Jane goes to the foot of the stairs and waits by the counter. When Patrick has taken up his position by the kettle she draws the newspaper out of her laundry bag and hands it to him.

He looks at her, not at the newspaper.

'Read it.'

Patrick scans the front page, 'Oh yes I saw that. It was a bit nasty, wasn't it? He was a piano-tuner or something.'

('"Ambassador of emotion",' he had said to her because somebody had said it to him – actually, one of his friends from the band – and he had liked it so much he wanted to share it with her. 'That's what we are . . . some of us. The proper musicians. "Ambassadors of emotion".')

Jane is looking at the photo-gallery. The shop bell rings. Patrick turns towards the man in the old Barbour jacket. Jane's eye is caught by a photo.

'I've some boxes in the car – would you take a look?' Behind the man with the patrician voice is a green Volvo estate with two wheels up on the pavement and its hazard lights flashing.

'Certainly,' Patrick says.

The man goes out and Jane watches Patrick follow him. Everything is gone now. Her mind is a blank.

Jane is standing at Alf's door with the newspaper and her paperback book in her hand. She knocks. The door opens as if he had been anticipating her knock. He has a clean, ironed, linen tea towel over his arm. He is wearing a white shirt, a grey sleeveless sweater and a burgundy tie. An apron is tied around his waist.

'Oh, it's you again,' Alf says.

'Can I come in?'

He stands aside and Jane walks in. The flat is neat and sparse, Alf's few possessions squared away in equally neat cupboards. An old aluminium pan with two potatoes in it boils on the two-ringed gas stove. The turbulent water is slicked with white starch. The windows, behind net curtains, are weeping with condensation. There are two pairs of black lace-up boots on a pristine sheet of newspaper on the sink drainer. Beside them is a tin of Kiwi boot polish and two brushes, their bristles in congress.

Alf gestures for Jane to sit down in one of the two armchairs. There is no settee. As she sits she notices the wedding photograph on the mantelpiece and another photograph: a studio portrait of two blond boys in blue school jumpers and grey shorts. She had assumed Alf to be childless. So far as she knows he is never visited. But the smiling grandchildren elicit no sympathy from her. She hands the newspaper to him together with the photograph from her book.

'Do I need my glasses for this?' Alf asks.

'. . . And you bought this on Tuesday you say?' Five minutes have passed. Alf is wearing his large glasses. The newspaper is on his knee. He's holding the paperback book in his right hand and the photograph in his left.

'Yes.'

'Well, I don't see there's much choice is there? I mean you should go to the police shouldn't you? That's evidence, that is.'

'What will they do?'

'Do? I don't know, love. I'm not a copper.'

'Well, what do you think?'

'I expect they'll take the photo and go to the bookshop and talk to the chappie in there and try and find out who sold him the book.'

'Will Patrick get into trouble?'

'Patrick?'

'At the bookshop.'

'Not unless he was the one who did it.'

'They'll take the photograph?'

'I should think so. Wouldn't you?'

Alf peers at the photo more closely. 'That's the what's-it's-name in the park, isn't it?'

Jane takes it back.

'You know – the temple?'

'Do you think if I asked them not to, they might just look at it and give it back to me?'

'I think that's possible, in the fullness of time.' Alf looks down at the newspaper again and rocks back to adjust his focal length. 'Lived not far from here, did he, according to this . . . Got a missus too – well I expect she's glad to know the body's been found. People say they prefer to know, don't they. Insurance and whatnot.'

'There's something else . . .'

'What?'

'I sold him the book.'

Alf removes his glasses and says, 'You what?'

'He gave it to me, John did, and I sold it to Patrick.'

'John who?'

'The man in the paper.'

'You knew the dead fellow?'

'Yes.'

'I see. Well that puts a different complexion on it. But if you sold it to . . . what was his name?'

'Patrick.'

'To Patrick, how come you've got it now?'

'I bought it back.'

'You what?'

'I go to Patrick's shop and if John's book is still there he still loves me.'

'. . . Right. And this is the fellow who's in the paper, is it?'

Jane stands and says 'Yes.'

None the wiser Alf hands her back the newspaper. 'Well, you be careful, all right?' he says.

9

Jane is approaching the park gates. Was there ever a time when park gates were locked shut? Certainly not in her lifetime. It is early afternoon and the place, as ever, is devoid of welcome. Jane passes the island of stunted saplings beyond the gateposts. An assaulted litter bin is perched at an angle on a grass verge bereft of grass. Further on, two police cars are parked just off the path and, thirty yards behind them, there's an incident van. It's like a circus of crime, Jane thinks, the circus of crime has come to town. When she is further along the track which leads to the boating lake she can see, far away to the left, a large, white tent among the trees. Jane peers at it, trying to remember what it reminds her of. Soon she realizes that it's not a memory at all, it just looks as though somebody has dropped a huge cube of light into the wood. A man in a pristine white coverall emerges from it and walks towards the vehicles like a spaceman flickering through the trees. A uniformed man waits patiently beside the tent. Static and conversation come in consecutive bursts from his radio. Jane will never be grown-up like the voices she hears. If the world blew up tomorrow she wouldn't care. There was a time when she would have done, but if somebody gave her a pill that would end it all for her and it didn't hurt she'd take it without hesitation.

'Without hesitation?' the finger-smeller had asked her.

'Well, except for Billy. Only I'm not much use to him any more.'

'Setting Billy aside – without hesitation?'

'Yes. Wouldn't you?'

'Do you consider yourself to be depressed?'

'I'm not the doctor.'

'Let me put it another way. If you had the means at hand, would you consider taking your own life?'

'What means?'

'I don't know. I would hardly imagine you'd expect me to list the most common . . .'

'A pill?'

'If that's how you . . .'

'Yes. Wouldn't everybody?'

'No, Jane. I don't believe that they would.'

'Why can't you kill yourself by holding your breath, then?'

'I don't know what you mean by that question.'

'If you could then everybody would.'

74

She had his full attention now. And how easy it had been; all that time she'd fought for it and he hadn't given it to her. All she'd had to do was to threaten to end it all. So her life did mean something. Now she was valued. 'Jane'. He had used her first name for a change and didn't even bother with the surname. She hated Hackett; all those jagged edges like a snowball with a stone in it. 'Hackett'. How ugly a name could be. Perhaps that's why her mother had dispensed with Tom – she'd used her husband's surname on him like a weapon.

'Wouldn't you?' Jane had asked the old psychiatrist. She liked him that day because he seemed harmless and one of the reasons was because he had tufts of grey hair sprouting from each ear.

'Me?' He hadn't been expecting that one but he should have been. It was a question he was often asked by his patients. For a moment he had dropped his guard and she'd got her answer: yes, he would. If he had a pill that would end his harmless life harmlessly, he'd take it. Because life was terribly hard and if death was dreamless sleep then who in their right minds wouldn't want it? Except on a bridge night. If it was a bridge night he'd save the pill for when he got home from the Conservative club. And then he'd have a large Scotch. Several large Scotches. A cigarette. He would buy a packet of Benson & Hedges for the occasion because he still missed smoking. But after the Scotch and the cigarettes he'd probably feel like sleeping – and when sleep was one of your few pleasures why deny yourself one more night of it? In the morning he would take the pill, when he awoke with the first cup of tea of the day. Or perhaps he would read the *Telegraph* first – and then . . . No, he wouldn't take the pill. Yes, of course life was hard, but there were sufficient small consolations littering his days to make it tolerable. The troubled young woman before him had no such pleasures because she had no resources of her own. She relied entirely on others to provide the moments which gave her life meaning. He found such people the hardest to help. His concern when he encountered them was to cover himself in his notes well enough so that when the inevitable did happen – and the suicide attempt succeeded, or more likely, was botched through incompetence – there would be nothing they could pin on him.

'You do realize, don't you . . .' he had said, 'that we'll have to keep you here for a while?'

'Why?'

'Well we can't have you doing . . . harm to yourself.'

'Who said anything about harm?'

The girl the nurses called the Sugar Plum Fairy had the bed next to Jane's in the ward. When they allowed her her own clothes she wore pink and lace. She had no wand or wings, but in Jane's mind's eye she did. At night, before lights out, she'd whisper to her: 'Remember, darling, cut down the arm, not across the wrist. Down the arm, not across.' And she'd laugh and go back to the book she was always reading. It was called *What Color Is Your Parachute?*

When she had been in there two weeks Jane had had a

revelation. It wasn't a hospital after all, she'd joined a cult and they were indoctrinating her, and once she had learned how to worship the new guru properly they'd allow her more freedom and eventually let her wander the streets again. Then she could act as a recruiter for them and bring in more people who could learn to be like her. She had never entirely rid herself of the belief.

'Life is not perfect,' he had told her. He was alive with love for her that night and said he wanted to tell her everything. He held her and danced with her around the room and he talked and talked for hours. 'Life is not perfect. So why make it a quest for perfection? Accept that and you can free yourself. You don't need to be any better than you are. It's OK to judge people. It's fine to hate. Just be the best you can be bothered to be and no better . . . and you'll be free.'

Three days later he left her and, although she pleaded with him, he wouldn't come back. It was for her, he said; he was leaving for her sake, before they got in too deep. What he didn't understand, Jane told him through her desperate tears, was that deep wasn't a matter of time, she was already in as deep as she could be so he might just as well stay with her. He smiled and said it was the same for him, but he had responsibilities, and it couldn't last. So it was best to end it all now before anybody got hurt.

'Mr Fancy Pants', the Sugar Plum Fairy called him. Or 'The Big I Am'. Jane could tell that the Sugar Plum Fairy didn't like what she heard about him so she stopped mentioning him so much, but sometimes she'd forget, or sometimes she didn't care.

'This is him,' the Sugar Plum Fairy said once, and Jane looked across at the page of a writing pad she was holding up. It said 'ME' in huge crude letters at the centre. 'And this is you.' She indicated a tiny, flowery 'you' in the bottom left-hand corner.

'And where are you?' Jane asked her.

'I'm on my own page.'

'Am I on your page too?'

'No, but be grateful you're in my book.'

Jane leaves the park path and uses the trees as cover from the rain. She has remembered to wear a mac. Today of all days, she is concentrating very hard on appearing normal. There must be ordinary women, she thinks, who would walk through the park in the rain on a day like this. Perhaps they would be using the park to cut off the corner. You could save ten minutes between the supermarket and the cinema if you went through the park. But what is showing at the Odeon? The last time she went as a treat but she couldn't bear it in there. It smelt of feet and the auditorium was too hot and the screen was barely larger than some of the televisions she saw in the windows of the electrical shops. It was a romance about a cheeky man who kept swearing, and there was very loud pop music all the way through it. Three young boys sitting in front of her were laughing all the time and throwing sticky sweets at a group of young girls. The sweets got caught in their hair.

But that wouldn't do. If they asked her why she was walking through the park she wouldn't use the cinema as an excuse, she'd just say she was out stretching her legs and hope they believed her.

Rain splashes down through the lush, green leaves. Jane looks at her shoes and sees that they are spattered with mud. Where she stands her weight has forced a pool of water from the ground. When she lifts her right foot the water soaks back in. A worm slithers out from a tunnel and slides down into another. When Jane sees worms she always wonders how they would taste. Not that she would ever put one in her mouth but it doesn't stop her wondering. It's part of the same feeling she gets when she sees foxes or squirrels – wanting to stroke them, or horses – wanting to pat their noses. Or sheep – wanting to run her fingers through their gritty, candy-floss fleeces. In fact it probably started with the sheep which were on the farm she once visited with her mother and father when she was very, very small. Almost her first memory: running her fingers through the thick fleece of a sheep. And remembering this, she knows that once upon a time they must have tried to be good parents.

Too late she realizes she has chosen the wrong shoes. They are her best ones – fabric, high heeled – but the mud has bled into the material. Very 'Molly', the Sugar Plum Fairy had once said of them and, when Jane had asked what she meant she said it was a term of appreciation usually applied to clothes or footwear – at least that's what she took it to mean. Jane decides she will just have to hope that the police won't interrogate her about her 'Molly' shoes. If they do she knows she'll probably end up in tears.

In the distance she can see the plastic tape of a crime-scene cordon.

Further on she arrives at the run-down stone folly. The temple is green with damp and age, the moisture from the floor of the woods is being soaked up by the pillars. She looks down at the picture in her hand then back at the folly. The photo has been taken in midsummer but the scene today looks only a little different; the light pressing down through the trees is less pristine.

Jane walks slowly towards the temple and goes inside. The structure is deep, the far end is in darkness. Hypodermic syringes and condoms litter the floor. The smell of urine is diluted by the dank winter smell of the woods. Jane stands beside a pillar, turns and looks back towards the trees. She hears a sharp sound behind her: the crack of thin plastic as a boot crushes a syringe. Slowly she turns. In the shadows is a figure. A man. Or a boy. However far they fall, women do not inhabit places like this.

'You looking for me?' the figure asks her. The voice is young but damaged by rough sleeping; there's an affected toughness in it. Jane doesn't reply. How could she answer such a question? Obviously she is not looking for him – why would she be?

'Well?' he presses.

'No. I'm looking for a friend.'

'I could be your friend.'

The shape shifts. The boy comes towards her, stumbling slightly; crouched. 'What do you think? Want to give it a go?' He stands there, swaying. He's close now: a young lad in an army jacket; pretty, lean and wasted with long dank hair held back in an Alice band.

'I don't think so.'

'Spare some change?'

'I haven't got any money.'

'Funny how people never have any money – I always used to have money in my pocket before – before circumstances got the better of me.'

'Well I don't.'

The youth takes a moment to look Jane up and down. He's trying to assess their relative positions in the world. He's always been shrewd, too shrewd perhaps. That's why he took to the drugs so easily: they stopped him having to vacuum up everybody's feelings. Having assessed Jane, he reaches the conclusion that they inhabit the same circle of hell. He relaxes. She is neither a threat nor a potential source of income. If anything, he feels sorry for her: another casualty of the NHS.

'It's all right. I'm quite harmless – to other people anyway.' The youth has an urge to talk to the girl: to tell her how he was going to be a doctor, how they fast-tracked him in languages and then sciences and it seemed there was nothing he couldn't do if he set his mind to it. He still uses his wits; in fact they're more useful to him now because they keep him alive. On bad days, of which there are many, he finds himself thinking of the sixth-form common room. Time and again his mind delivers him to that humid room; a riot of noise and the sweet sweat of adolescents and plastic cups of coffee from the machine, the *Velvet Underground* on the tinny stereo and laughter. Always laughter.

'So what are you doing here?' he asks her.

'I told you. I'm looking for a friend. He'll be here in a minute.'

He laughs. 'Really? You're not just sheltering from the rain?'

'No.'

The youth sees the photo in Jane's hand. 'That your friend is it?'

'Yes.'

'Let me see.'

'No.'

She turns away.

'Boyfriend is it?'

'Yes.'

'And you always carry his photo round, do you? Just so you don't forget his face?'

'. . . He's a piano-tuner.'

'Blind is he?'

'No.'

They circle each other.

'Strange place to meet on a day like this.'

'This was his place.'

'What, he lives here does he?'

'No.'

'You said it was his place. You mean it's not now?'

'No. Not now.'

'I've seen him here.'

'We never used to go where he lives.'

'Because?'

'She could never understand him the way I did.'

'Oh, he's married is he?'

'She made him do it, he didn't want to.'

'Weak then, is he?'

'No. He's sensitive.'

'Still, a piano-tuner, hardly the SAS is it?'

'He plays too. Played.'

'What?'

'Jazz and modern music. She did it. I know it was her.'

'Did what?'

'What do you think?'

'You've lost me.'

The youth is close to her now. He snatches the photo away from her.

'Give it back to me!'

He looks at it. She tries to grab it back – he turns away – she tries to reach around and snatch it. He takes a few steps towards the darkness. She follows him. They play cat and mouse in the shadows but she quickly loses patience and scratches the boy's face. With the pain of it, all the playfulness deserts him. He hits her hard in the mouth with a closed fist, drawing blood. Jane falls back to the floor –

shocked. The youth walks towards her and stands over her.

'I was going to be a doctor,' he tells her.

'I'm sorry.' Once she would have known what she needed to do or say to save herself, but now she has to rely on avoiding such situations. 'I'm sorry!'

'"Harmless, unless provoked." It's on my notes.'

Watching him carefully, Jane gets slowly to her feet and brushes down her clothes. 'I want my photograph back. Please.'

He looks at it again.

'Please!'

'Ten quid.'

'I told you I don't have ten pounds. I don't have any money.'

'No?'

He goes back into the shadows. She hears the strike of a lighter – the tiny flame illuminates the space around him. She glimpses a sleeping bag on the floor and an orange rucksack.

'Ten quid.'

'Please. I don't have . . . I can get it for you.'

'I don't believe you. You'll bring the police. Nice girl like you, attacked by a vagrant. Oh dear, that won't look good will it?'

'I'll do what you want. Anything you want.'

'Anything?'

'Anything.'

'No deal.'

He touches the lighter to the photo. She runs to him but the photo has caught, he drops it to the floor and soon there's nothing left of it.

'Never mind, love. Never mind.' He says as he slumps to his knees. The rush is gone.

In the pouring rain Jane is standing outside a police station looking up at the comforting white globes illuminating the mustard-stoned building. She's crying, but few would be able to differentiate the tears from the rain.

Inside, she goes to the counter, dripping. The officer behind the counter exchanges a look with his colleague. Eyebrows are raised to indicate the arrival of a regular customer.

Jane says: 'I'd like to report a theft . . .'

'Go on.'

'The theft of a photograph.'

'I see.'

'And a murder.'

'Blimey. Well you'd better come and sit down and tell us all about it, Jane.'

An hour later Jane is sitting with a blanket around her shoulders, shivering. She's drinking tea from a mug which she is holding between her two hands to draw from it all the warmth that she can. Two policemen and a policewoman are in hushed conversation behind her. When the door opens, another policeman comes in, followed by Alf. He's wearing a very damp cap and mac.

'Come on then, love, let's get you home.' Alf looks at the officers and smiles and shrugs.

'Tell them,' Jane implores.

'What?'

'Tell them about the photograph. They won't believe me.' She looks up at him.

'Photograph?' he says and laughs.

'Yes. You know. The photograph.'

'Oh, right. Yes, I've told them all about that.'

'And did they believe you, because I don't think they believe me.'

'Said they'd look into it.' He winks at the men.

'Why did you do that?'

'What?'

'You bastard.' Jane stands. The blanket falls away. She walks out of the police station. Alf follows at a short distance behind her as they return home.

Jane can hear Alf banging on her door with the palm of his hand.

'Come on love, open up,' he calls. 'I know she's in there,' Jane hears him say to Maude as she comes to join him.

'What's the matter with her?' Maude asks Alf.

'Something's upset her.'

'She's young. Girls of her age are always upset about something.'

'Yeah . . .'

'Are you all right, dear?' Maude calls.

'She won't answer. I've been trying for nigh on five minutes.'

'Well perhaps she doesn't want your help.'

'Maybe not.'

'. . . I thought we might go out.'

'Did you?'

'Yes. If you wanted to ask me.'

'What about her?'

'She'll survive.'

Inside the flat Jane continues to sit at the kitchen table in the dark. She's watching the woman in the building behind hers, washing up at the kitchen sink. The woman is wearing pink rubber gloves and staring unhappily into space as she works. She breaks off to scratch her nose with the inside of her wrist. Jane takes a pair of scissors from the drawer, goes into the bedroom and sits on the bed. She picks up the newspaper and cuts out the photo of the piano-tuner on the front page. She then returns to the drawer, gets out the small plastic container of drawing-pins and pins the newspaper cutting to the wall.

'Where are you?' she says towards the photo. '. . . Are you there?' she calls. She listens but there's no reply.

The newsprint is fading, the photograph seems curiously lifeless.

10

Jane is in a glass phone-booth. An indeterminate time has passed. In that time she has completed no tasks; she has eaten no food, taken no drink, held no conversations, read nothing, watched no television, listened to no radio, written no letters, attempted no word-search games, said no prayers, told no lies, felt no fear. She has walked no dog, doodled on no newspapers, hummed no tunes, nor has she washed her hair, showered, bathed, or looked at the sky and seen faces in the clouds. She has wrapped no presents, peeled no fruit, iced no cakes, made no speeches about her life to rooms full of people who don't seem to be listening. No bird has flown above her, she has walked down no dark tunnels, washed no whites whiter, talked to no ghosts. Because she cannot drive she has attempted no three-point turns, a manoeuvre which Hackett always said defeated her mother, even though he liked watching her skirt rise up her thighs as she tried to turn the car around in the narrow street. ('Nice thighs, your mother, just like yours, Janey, just like yours.') She has neither crossed her thighs nor parted them. But she has been occupied by thoughts of her son, whom she remembers she called Billy, not William, because she didn't want anybody to shorten his name.

And why was that?

The reason, as it was suggested to her by the woman doctor, was that she had had some premonition that she would ultimately lose any influence she had over him. She had therefore chosen the name Billy so that, in this at least, her mark on him would always remain. Jane had accepted this reading at the time. With the woman doctor it was even more necessary to go along with her assessments. She seemed to take criticism very personally, and when Jane once asked her if she, herself, was unhappy, the woman had stormed out of the room.

This is how it had ended with Billy: she had been in hospital again and Billy had been looked after by the woman next door. Jane called it 'next door' out of habit; it was actually the other flat at the top of the three-storey block. The dwellings were stacked in pairs; each pair of flats shared an open landing and a coal bunker which was used as the repository of black bin bags. Scattered between the blocks, which were spread randomly about a bleak, grassy mound at the edge of the town, were a number of piles of broken washing machines, dishwashers and fridges. Two months before, the council had begun the clean-up operation and had got as far as assembling the piles of decommissioned electrical equipment. Since then, work on the project had ceased and the estate looked like an abandoned military camp awaiting the bulldozers.

In the winter, the rain and wind drove through the open landings. In the summer, when there had been no wind for a few days, the landings stank and the mice came out. The woman next door to Jane had four children of her own, three dogs which fouled the steps, and a husband who worked nights. Clive had tattoos on his shoulders and a cheeky charm which he no longer wasted on his wife. He often came around to invite Billy out to play football with him. Jane found it awkward when Clive called because Billy didn't like football (the only one of Clive's children who was old enough to play properly was a harelipped girl with a runny nose who didn't show any interest). But Jane felt obliged to let Billy go with him because Clive's wife, Sharon, helped her out, and her lending Billy to Clive seemed to even up the debt. But Jane knew this wasn't as straight-forward as it seemed. She was aware that Clive came around because he fancied her, and, in terms of childcare, each time Clive took Billy out, her childcare debt to the couple increased. But Clive's charm had a way of winning her over. She couldn't have refused him anything, and in that respect Jane recognized he was like Hackett; a man who gave the appearance of doing you a favour even though it was you who was doing him one. However tangled the obligations, on the surface it seemed as though he was the one who was putting himself out. It was a rare gift.

Sharon never complained about her life to Jane. Like many people in desperate circumstances, she spent what little surplus energy she had in helping those who were better off than she was. So, although Jane struggled to maintain her equilibrium and sometimes didn't have sufficient money to get by, her life in some respects was easier. She therefore felt guilty when Sharon offered to mind Billy when she went in for her appointments, and guiltier still when she ended up in hospital and her freedom was again removed from her. There was no family to help out (at least not one she was in contact with), so Sharon became what her mother would have called 'a godsend'. When she did come out of the hospital after her longer stays, Billy's clothes were filthy and he would always have lost weight. But he seemed so grateful to see her again that she didn't have the heart to ask him how well he'd been looked after.

What Billy didn't tell her was that when Clive called around it wasn't for football. Instead, he took him to The Bugle, a low-rise 1960s pub on the edge of the estate where he made him sit in the paved beer-garden until he'd finished his afternoon's drinking and pool-playing. Through the filthy window, Billy would watch Clive leaning over the beer-stained green baize, a cigarette always in his mouth, part of his attention on the game, the rest of it on the barmaid who seemed to spend an equal proportion of her time looking at him. One day Billy had jumped with shock because the back door of the pub had burst open and Clive and the barmaid had come barging through it, their lips clamped together, tugging at each others' clothes. The barmaid had fumbled open the door of the wooden shed where they kept the sun umbrellas and the Calor-gas patio warmers and they had fallen inside. Billy heard them bumping around in there for ten minutes before they came out again.

Billy didn't tell his mother about the pub visits because, the first time they went out, Clive had said to him that he would hurt him if he did. Even without the threat, Billy would never have told Jane what went on; even at that young age, he believed that he bore the responsibility for his mother's happiness. It was a burden he was happy to shoulder because it made him feel he had a purpose. And throughout the dark weeks he spent with the family next door while his mother was in hospital, he knew he had to stay strong for her. He therefore didn't mention the squalor, the rows, the lack of food, the smell he once identified as a dead hamster under a settee and the fact that he had to accept the continuing charity of a teacher because she recognized that he had neither dinner money nor a packed lunch.

It was the teacher who betrayed him.

'I'll have to say something, Billy,' she had said, kneeling down so they were face-to-face in the hot classroom. He could see her reel back a little when she caught a draught of the smell of him but she continued fussing at his shirt buttons.

'No.'

'It's for your own good.'

'She won't come back.'

'She will, Billy. It won't affect your mum. They may just have to look a little more closely at where you stay when she's not there.'

The teacher was pretty and delicate and smelt of flowers, but she wasn't as pretty as his mother. Nobody was. And he hated her after that because, soon after their conversation, people started turning up unannounced at the flat: first a woman and a man came one evening, then two men who poked around and opened the cupboards, and looked inside the fridge and even the laundry basket. It was shortly after that visit that he was taken away. In his mind he decided that it was what they saw in there that caused it.

Billy knew that whatever he faced in his life from then on, he would never feel as bad as the day he was taken away by the woman and the man in the car. It took him weeks to forget the face of his mother on the open landing, looking down on him as he was led into the car. A man was holding her back to stop her running after him. She was beyond hysteria. He made himself not cry because he knew it would only make it worse for her. He swore, however, that one day he would return to his mother. Wherever they made him go, one day they would be back together.

'Never make the mistake of believing,' the Sugar Plum Fairy once whispered to Jane in the hospital, 'that those who work here are without fault. Most of them are more fucked-up than we are: the only difference is that they get paid for being in here and we don't.'

Jane wished she could trust the Sugar Plum Fairy more. Sometimes she felt she really knew her and they were in it together. At other times she seemed to be on the side of the nurses and the doctors. Jane was sure that the Sugar Plum Fairy reported what she had said back to them, but because she had nobody else to confide in, sometimes she had no choice but to tell her what she was feeling. She would never have betrayed her to the doctors whatever they promised her. But, all in all, Jane thought, it was worth it if only to have somebody to walk around the wards with or to stand next to in the car park and watch the world go by on the other side of the barrier. If she had a real friend she knew it would be like this only better: she would have the companionship but she would also have the trust.

How fortunate people were who could find other people who would like them enough to be proper friends. And it must, Jane knew, be a failing in her that she'd never really managed it. Perhaps she was too demanding. Perhaps people didn't like her moods or the way she looked. It was a shame, really, because Jane felt that she had a lot to offer the right person: she would be loyal, and she'd help them clean up if they needed it, and if they had a cold she'd go to the shop for them and buy them some medicine. She would feed their cat or look after their dog if they went away. She'd even pick up the poop and put it in a bag in the dog-shit bin.

She'd never forget a birthday, and on bonfire night she'd tell them which hill was the best one to stand on so that you could see the whole town and all the firework displays for free.

'What?' the Sugar Plum Fairy said.

'What?' Jane said back.

'Firework displays. What are you talking about?'

'Nothing. Is it good – that book?' Jane asked her.

'I don't know. I keep reading the same page over and over again. I just can't seem to stop myself.'

So the Sugar Plum Fairy had put her book down and they had both gone outside (with permission) to the covered area by the car park so that she could have a ciggy. Jane had a drag but at that time she hadn't taken to cigarettes. While they sat together the schools ended for the day and the pavement beyond the hospital fence suddenly became full of swarming children. The Sugar Plum Fairy was prompted by this to ask Jane about Billy because Jane kept Billy's photograph with her at all times. Jane told her about the time when Billy had just turned six, not long before he went away, and he had asked if he could have a friend for tea.

'That's nice,' the Sugar Plum Fairy said. She approved of stories which illustrated children being kind to other children.

'No,' Jane said. 'No. It wasn't nice.'

'No?'

And because it wasn't the old psychiatrist or the young

one, and because the Sugar Plum Fairy was genuinely interested in why it hadn't been nice, Jane had told her:

'I saved some fish fingers . . . We didn't have much money. In fact I think that was the day after Jim took ten pounds out of my purse without telling me. He said he wanted to come round and see Billy and all he wanted. Well . . .'

'Your husband?'

'No. We weren't married. He worked in a factory making wooden pallets. But, even when we were together I never called him there, not even in emergencies. He said I wasn't to because the women from the office would take the mickey when he walked through the factory to come to the phone.'

'He sounds like a typical man.'

'I went there once because it was his birthday and I just wanted to go in and wish him happy birthday properly and give him his present because he'd left before I woke up.'

'What did you buy him?

'I got him a beer tankard and got his name engraved on it and it said 'Mm, Beer', underneath. But I was going to give it to him that night. Anyway I'd got him some tobacco as well and a new pouch for it – I knew he was short – so I took it there but they wouldn't let me in.'

'Who wouldn't?'

'There was a man on the gate.'

'Did you tell him who you were?'

'I said I was with Jim, and he said "Join the queue". I thought Jim might have been proud of me turning up there.'

'What happened to him?'

'He went up north.'

'. . . And this was the day Billy was having a friend for tea?'

'Oh, yes.' And Jane felt sick again, just as she had that afternoon when Billy had come out of school wearing the coat that was too big for him and with his satchel slung over his shoulder even though none of the other kids did that. He had seen her straight away, and came over but then continued past her, walking towards the school gate, expecting her to follow him. And when she had caught him up and asked him about the boy who was supposed to be coming for tea, Billy had said, 'Can't come.' And then Jane had seen the boy's mother in a group by the gates. She had been talking to two other mothers but kept breaking off to look towards her; it was obvious they were talking about her, so she had gone up to them and asked the woman why her son couldn't come.

'We don't make him do anything he doesn't want to. As a mother, I'm sure you can understand that, can't you?' the woman had said.

'You mean he doesn't want to come to tea with my Billy?' Jane had said, just for the want of something to say; to stop herself from saying anything hurtful to the bitch.

'No. He doesn't want to come to tea with your Billy.' She stressed 'tea' as though it was a word she never used herself. Somebody laughed. And then she turned away and Jane had to look hard for Billy because he had wandered too far away from her and she had been afraid she'd lost him in the crowd.

'We had the fish fingers anyway,' she told the Sugar Plum Fairy, who by now was crying.

'And what did Jim say?'

'Oh, he was always back late when he stayed over. He would have said I was just being too sensitive or something.'

Evenings with Billy were the happiest times of her life. He was her little soldier, was Billy. This is what they would do: they would have tea together, each with their own tray on their knee. They'd turn off the top light and sit side-by-side on the settee and watch television. Billy would choose the channel, and then, when that programme ended, she'd have her choice. But they wouldn't really be watching, they'd be talking, even though they were looking at the television all the time. Sometimes they'd go for two or three minutes between a question and an answer because something had caught their attention on the screen. And when Billy went to bed she'd always tuck him in tight and kiss him on the fore-head and then on each cheek. After that she'd take his little round glasses off and put them on his bedside table. It was a ritual they had, just as it was for Billy to tell her exactly how far she should close the door so that the light from the hallway came just a little way into his room. 'Bit more . . . bit more. No, too much. That's enough.'

'"That's enough",' she told the Sugar Plum Fairy. 'That was always the last thing he said at night: "That's enough". And I'd whisper: "Love you, Billy. I love you so much, my darling."'

'Why don't you get him back?' the Sugar Plum Fairy had

asked her, but Jane hadn't been able to tell her about the court and what they said because remembering the day the boy didn't come home for tea had set her off again. She didn't really come back to her senses for three weeks, by which time she seemed to have lost a stone in weight, her hair needed washing and she had a bruise on the top of her leg where they had stuck a needle into her to calm her down. But that was the start of it all – the day the boy didn't come home for tea.

11

Jane dials the mobile number Ian the plumber has given her but the phone is switched off so she tries the maintenance company she used the first time she called him out. She tells the man who answers that she needs Ian's home number. 'He's . . . he left some of his tools at the flat . . .' she explains, but the man doesn't believe her, she can tell, because he says he's not authorized to give out phone numbers. She tells him he's talking to her like she's demanding the private number of the Prime Minister. The man says he can see her point, but he says he still can't give her the number. As a compromise, however, (he uses the word 'however') he'll contact Ian himself and ask him to call her direct. Can he have her number? She tells him she doesn't have one; she can't afford a mobile, even a pay-as-you-go, but she will wait in the phone-box and he can call her there.

The man on the phone tells her it's a myth that pay-as-you-go is cheaper than contract, and he should know because his daughter-in-law works for one of the phone companies. Jane explains that, like electricity, she can't afford big bills when they come in. She'd rather know exactly where she is, as far as money is concerned. He seems disappointed that his advice has gone unheeded, but is glad to have reached out to her across the night. She seems edgy; fractious. If she was his daughter he'd be around there like a shot, pub quiz-night or no pub quiz-night.

She puts down the phone and goes out of the booth to get away from the smell of piss and wet newspaper. Across the road Alf and Maude, dressed up in funeral clothes, are walking arm-in-arm towards The Constant Service pub.

Jane waits for an hour and a half but Ian the plumber does not call. She rings his mobile number fifteen times, but the phone is always switched off and an unfailingly polite woman offers to divert her call to the Orange answering service. Finally, after running out of 20p coins, she returns to her flat.

The kitchen in the flat behind Jane's is lit but empty. She looks at the clock on the wall. 10 p.m. 11.15. 11.25. The front door bangs. She leaps to her feet and goes to the door and looks down the stairwell, but it's just Alf and Maude back drunk from the pub. Alf grabs the banister and begins to haul himself up the stairs. He offers his hand back to Maude as though he is going to tug her up a steep hill. When he catches sight of Jane he nudges Maude, who looks up too. They giggle. Jane goes down the stairs, past them, without her coat and out into the night.

'Where you off to?' Alf calls after her, stupefied by drink.

Jane is in the phone-booth again: '. . . Well that's not good enough,' she is saying, 'I thought you were supposed to be a 24-hour company, that's how you advertise yourself . . . no, I don't want another plumber, I want to see the man who came the night before last . . . yes, and he said I should call him on his mobile but it's switched off . . . Yes, he did . . . I've got some of his tools and he said . . . he said if I needed to get him back at any time he'd come out . . .'

There's a new voice on the other end of the phone now. The 'however' man has gone out to his pub quiz and he hasn't passed on her message to the man who is now taking the calls. The new man tells her he is sorry but he is contracted by a number of plumbing and electrical companies who all divert their phones to him after 9 p.m. and he sits up all night and answers them. Jane can hear the hush and roar of a football crowd on the television in his tiny room. She can visualize it: the full ashtray and empty beer cans, the take-away containers and yesterday's Sun, but her mind stops short of imagining whether the man works from home or has taken a small room in an office block or an industrial estate. Perhaps he has even sub-let some space from a taxi firm. The lives of those who work at night have always intrigued her. She has always considered herself to be more at home in the night than in the day. One day, she imagines, when the world is too full, people will choose between being night- or day-people and live in shifts. The shops will always be open, and when one person gets up, another will come back in and sleep in their bed. It goes without saying that she would put herself down for being a night-person – and then she wouldn't ever have to see or be seen again in the sunlight – and that would suit her down to the ground.

Jane tries a new tack. She explains to the man that she is concerned that the boiler will explode and, upon hearing this, the man pays attention and, almost immediately, offers her Ian the plumber's home phone number.

'Wait a minute,' Jane says and traps the phone beneath her ear as she once saw a woman on TV do. She writes the number down on a piece of paper she has remembered to bring along for the purpose. 'Thank you,' she says and puts down the phone. While the night-man goes back to his chicken korma, she dials the number he has given her. A woman answers and Jane considers that the telephone must have brought her only good news because of the bright way she says: 'Hello.' Nowadays nobody answers with their telephone number. When Jane was young, everybody did.

'. . . Yes, hello,' Jane says, and then wonders if she should have given the call more thought. What should she call him? 'I'd like to speak to Ian please,' she says, thinking that he could easily have given her his name while he was mending the boiler. If his wife thought that was too forward of him then she'd just have to apologize to him later. But she was sure he'd understand because what she needed him for was more important: she needed him to tell her what to say to make the police believe her.

'Can I tell him who's calling?' The woman is already suspicious but she is maintaining her politeness because any call is a potential source of business for her husband.

'Yes, it's Jane . . . Hackett,' she says and then gives her address because an address adds to the formality. '. . . He did a job on my boiler and I think there's something wrong with it.'

'I see,' the woman says, stalking the borders of her territory now. 'It's very late.'

'I know, but he said I should call and say . . .' What was it he had told her to say? Was she supposed just not to say anything — she really couldn't remember. 'He said I should call and say the boiler was broken and it was an emergency.'

'He said that, did he?'

'Yes. I think . . . I don't know.'

'You don't know what he said you should say?'

'Yes. No.'

'You don't seem to know what you want do you?'

'Well . . .'

'We're talking about my Ian, are we?'

'Yes. Your Ian. Is that his name?'

'You tell me. That's what you called him.'

'Ian. Yes, I think he said his name was . . .'

'And would you just like to tell me, just so's I can tell Ian, exactly what's happened to your boiler.'

'It's gone out. The light inside. The pilot light's gone out.'

'Oh. It's gone out has it – the pilot light?'

Jane can hear another voice behind the woman's now; a deep voice offering calming words because the pitch of the woman's voice on the other end of the phone has become shrill. The warm fuzz of Ian is in the room. Now Jane remembers: Ian had told her his wife's name: Donna. That was it. And Jane had said to him that she hadn't known a Donna, and he said let's keep it that way. He also suggested she should apologize for disturbing her.

'I'm sorry for calling so late, Donna.' There, she had done what he had told her to do.

'What!' Donna says. 'How do you . . . who are you?'

'I'm Jane. Hackett. I told you.'

'You're a fucking bitch, that's what you are. And if I–'

Jane hears the phone fall and Ian's voice clearly now, and Donna's piercing accusation. And then something is thrown and breaks against the wall, and it sounds as though a wild beast has been let loose in the room. Then the sound becomes muffled, the line cuts and Jane is left listening to the dialling tone. She looks at the receiver but all she can see is a heavy plastic handset tethered to a silver block by a piece of armour-plated flex. The handset is heavy. It could be used as a cosh if you got somebody close enough to it.

A minicab driver passes the phone-box and sees the woman inside staring at the phone. Under the white light she looks like a high-class tart in a TV drama, he thinks as he accelerates away.

When Jane walks through the front door of the house Alf is waiting for her, sitting at the foot of the stairs in his jacket and coat. The knot of his tie is slightly loosened.

'You shouldn't be out on your own at this time of night, love. I was set to call in the old Bill.' The drink in his blood-stream has slowed his thoughts. Jane can see that he is working hard at making sense.

'You don't care.'

'It might not seem like that, but I do.'

He stands stiffly. His job is done.

'I saw you going out. With Maude.'

'Yeah. Well we went for a couple to The Service.'

'Did you have a nice time?' Jane asks him, accusingly.

'It wasn't so bad.'

'I've never been.'

'I don't think it's your sort of place.'

Jane begins to cry. She doesn't quite know why but she thinks it might be because she doesn't know anybody well enough to ask them out for a drink to The Constant Service. Perhaps Patrick would come with her one night if she offered to pay. She would have to save up for a few weeks. But she wouldn't know what to do when she went in. Would she go to a table with Patrick and then give him her purse to take up to the bar – or would they go up to the bar together and when they reached it would she ask him what he wanted? She always remembered what Hackett said when he took her mother to pubs: he said he didn't want her standing at the bar like a common tart. Hackett saw visions of hell everywhere and so does Jane. She can read faces like her father could. If she walked up the aisle of a bus she could tell you the story of every man, woman and child she passed. She has to stop herself because that way madness lies.

Alf approaches her but he doesn't feel he knows her well enough to embrace her and, even through the sad confusion she's feeling, she doesn't trust him enough to collapse onto him, which is all she really wants to do.

'Come on, love,' he cajoles and his impotence touches her and makes her feel guilty for showing off her misery. Alf's careworn face can no longer pretend anything beyond what it feels. He's glad when Jane slinks away up the stairs like a wounded animal. He hears her door open and close, a disembodied voice from the second floor, a bath emptying and a telephone trilling. He goes out of the house and breathes deeply of the cold, damp air outside.

Jane does not turn on the light straight away. Instead she goes to the kitchenette and looks out across the short distance into the kitchen of the flat behind hers. The room is empty, the light is off, but the cabinets on the wall are illuminated by the grey, dancing glow from a nearby television. Jane's window is ruled by the faint lines of a Venetian blind. She turns the flimsy plastic wand and the sticky slats seal themselves together making a barrier against the night. Turning away, she goes to the bedroom where she sits on the bed. For the first time she feels the dampness of her clothes. She shivers and looks towards the wardrobe to check if her dressing gown is hanging on the door. But the louvre doors are shut, the dressing gown is inside and the effort required to get herself from the bed to the wardrobe is too great. She hugs herself and feels some comfort. Hunched forward slightly she finds that some heat is released from the pit of her stomach and the cold retreats. A door bangs shut along the corridor; a careless slam not a pointed or angry one. Someone has returned home drunk: Carey, perhaps, or Frankie. She feels the need for the proximity of people but she can't find it in herself to leave the flat and go to the 24-hour supermarket. She makes a great effort to stop herself going through the telephone call with Donna. It has touched her in a way she thought she was incapable of feeling. But then the young doctor would have immediately identified the reason: she would have told Jane that it was to do with the sense of abandonment she has always had.

This is how it ended with her mother and father: after the train journey to Skegness and the chilling week they spent there as a family in which she had to try and sleep on a settee while her mother and father made noises in the bed, they told her she might have to go and live somewhere else for a while. They seemed to believe that by couching the move as possible rather than inevitable it would make it easier for her. But she recognized that the 'might' was to save their feelings and not hers.

'Just until we get sorted out, Janey, love,' her father had said.

'Won't be for ever,' her mother had promised.

Both of them had therefore lied from the beginning.

And so they helped her pack her case. She was aware of the looks that were passing between them and the barely concealed tears on her father's face (though not her mother's). And when her mother held up her teddy bear, her father had to leave the room. A moment later she could smell him smoking in the lavatory. Her mother laid the teddy bear on the soft pillow of her clothes in the suitcase, and then forced it closed.

'Come on now,' she cajoled, picking up the case and holding out her other hand for Jane to take. But the suitcase was too heavy so she left it in Jane's bedroom and called to Hackett to fetch it down when he'd finished in the lavatory.

She held Jane's hand all the way to the car, which Jane liked. Hackett followed them after he'd locked the front door. He looked unkempt, his suit jacket was unbuttoned, as was his waistcoat; his trousers looked as if they needed pressing. It was late afternoon and the last thing Jane carried with her from her home was the sight and sound of a bird singing on the telegraph wire outside her bedroom. She saw it when she looked out of the back window of the car as they drove her away. Something told her she would never be going back to that place, but nothing prepared her for never seeing her mother and father from that day on.

Some time into the night Jane hears knocking at the front door. It disturbs her sleep but she constructs a dream around it to explain it away. When the persistence of it forces her to abandon sleep she discovers that she has got herself into bed, fully-clothed. She is surprised that she has slept because the top light in her bedroom is still on and the bare bulb gives off a harsh white light. She looks at the clock on the radio: 3.07 a.m. She gets out of bed and goes down the stairs to the front door and opens it to Ian the plumber who has a red holdall in his right hand. He doesn't say anything because he considers that nothing needs to be said, but Jane does not like the assumption he is making: that she will let him in so that he can stay the night with her. Particularly as the look he gives her is one of such hatred that she feels she owes him nothing. They face each other – her intransigence matching the force of his anger.

'Are you going to let me in then?' Ian the plumber asks her. If he hadn't said anything, she could have held out, but she can't stand up to such a simple request. After all, it was what she'd wanted all along, wasn't it? Ian the plumber had come around to see her. She stands aside and he bullies his way up the stairs and then into her room. Because it's not yet his territory he stands in the centre of the small living room waiting to be told what to do. Just as Jane is about to tell him, his mobile phone rings. He darts a hand to it, scans the number, thumbs the accept button and clamps the phone to his ear saying, 'Hello, doll.' He pushes past Jane and goes out into the corridor, tugging the door shut behind him. Jane listens as he pleads and cajoles. When the volume of his voice reduces she realizes that he is not talking more quietly but retreating along the corridor. Finally the voice is silent. Moments later she hears rapid footsteps, her door is pushed open and Ian the plumber faces her. He is flushed and spent and seems to want to hit her. Instead, he waves a finger in her face and tells her: 'Stay out of my life – all right? Just stay away. And hers. If you call again I'll come here and I'll fucking do you – all right? I mean it. I'll . . . I'll twat you.'

'Yes,' Jane says. 'I understand.'

When Ian the plumber has gone, she screams. Finally, gratefully, she screams. He is gone. Dead. She is alone.

Jane wakes in her bed. The curtains are so thin it is light in the room. She hears sounds from the kitchen. She blinks the sleep from her eyes and sits up and calls: 'John?'

Maude appears at the bedroom door with a cup of tea and says: 'Good morning, dear.'

'Have you been here all night?' Jane asks her.

'No. Alf sat up with you until after five and he asked me to pop and see you this morning.'

'I don't remember.'

'How are you feeling?'

'Feeling?' No worse or better than the way she always feels in the morning. The same blank space in her mind where her yesterday used to be. She would reconstruct it, slowly, as she bathed or ate her toast, but sometimes the details eluded her. Today she could remember having been in a phone-booth and then feeling cold and shivery, but only then did she recall Ian the plumber's visit. Had he hit her? She didn't think so.

'Thank you,' Jane says as Maude hands over a cup of tea. Jane is now aware of the pungent smell of cigarette smoke in the flat.

'I think you worried Alf, but then it's very easy to worry men, isn't it? They don't understand . . . I mean a number of the gentlemen I've known have accused me of being potty. I'm not potty, I always told them, I'm a woman – and women are mysterious creatures. Aren't we?' she smiles brightly and surveys the room. '. . . Well, I've tidied round a bit and I'll leave you to get dressed. Just knock if there's anything you need.'

'Tidied?' This alarms Jane because now she draws a line between the night and the evening, and traces it back further: she wanted Ian the plumber to come around to help her decide what to tell the police because they hadn't believed her when she told them about the photograph of the man she found in the book whose body foxes had found in the wood. The photograph was all she had of him. It was in her copy of *Pierre et Jean* that she would take back to the bookshop time and time again and leave it there for a week, two weeks, until she would return and buy it back. And nobody could understand why she needed to do it over and over again. But the photograph had been burned and now all she had of him was his picture in the newspaper.

Jane scrambles out of bed and goes to the kitchen. There is no sign of the newspaper.

'Where did you put it?' she asks Maude.

'What?'

'The paper.'

'Well I . . . put it out, I mean the bin men are coming today and I assumed. . .'

Outside they hear the air-breaks of a bin lorry. Jane dashes downstairs and out of the front door. The huge communal bin is clamped in the pincers of the lorry and is being slowly upended. A trickle of foul water and debris becomes a tumbling, stinking, wet mass.

'Stop!' Jane shouts.

The man operating the pincers can't hear. Jane runs up to him, sees the big red switch, hits it and stops the machine. The soggy mess of litter has been dropped into the back of the lorry. She plunges her arms in. She has forgotten that she cut out the photograph and pinned it to the wall.

Jane is in the bath. The steam in the room is thick – she believes that she can see a figure through it, sitting on a chair in the bathroom.

The figure says: '. . . You understand? . . . Do you understand what I'm saying to you?'

'You said you loved me . . .'

'Yeah, I know I said that but . . .'

'Well I don't understand why I can't call you then.'

'I explained all that to you. I have responsibilities.'

'So what are you doing here?'

No answer.

'Well?' she presses.

'I can't stop myself.'

Somebody bangs on the door and a harsh woman's voice tells her she's been in there for two hours.

'There's others in here need to use it, you know, you're not the bloody queen of the jungle.' Jane looks up at the green painted walls, the white tiles, the grab rail for the mobility-impaired, the alarm cord hanging from the ceiling and realizes with horror where she is, again.

12

Billy knows something is wrong because nobody will confirm the date on which he will see his mother. When the day of their quarterly meeting arrives and passes he withdraws to his bedroom, but it is only three days later when he begins to refuse food that Fiona and Don again call in the support worker. She arrives wearing the same blue blouse she wore on her last visit. Billy notices this when, from his bedroom window, he watches her get out of her Fiat Punto. Fiona has tried to turn the event into a party. She feels that if they can find something to celebrate in the evening then the awfulness of the situation will be alleviated. The woman had refused Fiona's offer of a meal, but when she is lead through into the living room by Don, Fiona goes to the kitchen and takes from the oven a selection of vol-au-vents, sausage-rolls, and scampi in breadcrumbs. She has provided cocktail sticks for the scampi; she will encourage the woman to eat the other pastries with her fingers. The informality will, she believes, break the ice.

She tries to hear what the woman is saying to Don as she transfers the heated pastries from a pristine oven tray onto an octagonal white plate. Although she can pick up the tone, which is jovial enough, she cannot make out the words.

'I've just warmed up some . . .' she says, entering the room. Don stands up. An awkward man at the best of times, most social events leave him floundering. The visitor looks at the plate with what she hopes signals enthusiasm.

'You really shouldn't have . . .' she says, sitting up a little straighter on the settee. She has arranged to meet a colleague for a meal later in the evening and calculates the minimum number of pastries she can eat without seeming rude.

'It's nothing really. Just a few bits and pieces . . .' Fiona says. Continuing to hold the plate in her left hand she attempts, with her right, to lift the flap of the gateleg table. Don looks on until Fiona fires a sharp instruction at him which prompts him to take the plate from her. Convention dictated that it should have been he who set up the table, leaving Fiona with the plate, but she holds her irritation in check, reinstates her smile, and offers the woman a paper plate, and then a serviette. The transaction is stage-managed by smiles and takes place in silence.

When the woman has helped herself to one sausage-roll and one piece of scampi, Don inspects the selection on the octagonal plate. Party food is a rare treat in this household.

Contemplating the choice on offer, he momentarily forgets that a visitor is in the room, and it is only when the silence goes on for too long that he looks up to see Fiona staring at him. Immediately he knows he has failed to fulfil another of his obligations and that he will feel the full force of his wife's anger when the woman has gone. He must remember not to smile when she shouts at him the next time because it just makes her shout more and slap him. He takes the nearest pastry, a serviette, a cocktail stick and sits obediently beside the woman on the settee. Don is allowed the company of other women only in the safety of his own house. On the rare occasions he and Fiona go out to the pub on a Saturday night, he is careful to use his wife as a barrier between himself and any stray woman. At such times, Fiona's habit is to engage him in intense conversation, which precludes him from communicating with anybody else in the room. He knows that she isn't the least bit interested in talking to him, she is merely signalling her control over him. He recognizes that he will never understand her and will often disappoint her, but he consoles himself with the thought that she is a woman and all women are a closed book to him.

'Well,' the visitor says. Ten minutes have passed, sufficient time for the pleasantries to be over. 'Perhaps you could tell me how William has been since we last spoke.'

'William?' Don says, as if the nature of the woman's visit has only just occurred to him.

'He doesn't talk to us any more,' Fiona says.

'Not at all?'

'Rarely. And now he's not eating.'

The woman nods.

'Is he, Don?'

'No. Well . . . put it this way. He's not been eating here.' Don smiles broadly at the woman, indicating a suspicion he has shared with Fiona: that William has been eating elsewhere.

'Oh, Don, for heaven's sake . . .' Fiona says. She puts her paper plate onto the floor, wipes her fingers on the serviette, goes to the lounge door and closes it. 'Do you see what I have to put up with?' she asks the woman.

'Well, love, he's a lad, and you know what lads get up to.'

'No. I don't, Don,' Fiona says. 'Why don't you tell us?'

Don smiles at the woman in apology, but he can't maintain eye contact with her.

Fiona continues. 'He's not eating and he's not talking to us. That's what he's getting up to. And I'm . . . I'm getting a bit tired of it if the truth be told.'

The woman puts her plate onto the gateleg table, grateful for the excuse to rid herself of it.

'OK,' she says. 'So he's not communicating with you at all?'

'No,' Fiona says. Don shakes his head. He eyes the octagonal plate but decides that now is not the time to help himself to another sausage-roll. He's not sure about the scampi; they seemed a bit cold in the middle and tasted of too much lemon juice.

'And what about school? Is he still attending?'

'As far as we know,' Fiona says.

'Oh, he's going to school,' Don says. 'I mean they'd tell us, wouldn't they, if he wasn't?' Perhaps if he stretched over, he could pick up the plate and offer the woman another helping. Then he could take one for himself as he put the plate down. That way Fiona wouldn't be able to criticize him.

'It's difficult,' the woman says. 'But the first thing I think you should know is that this is not your fault.' She looks first at Fiona, then at Don to make sure they have both heard. Fiona returns her look in grateful silence while Don reaches for the plate of food.

Twenty minutes after the woman arrives, Billy hears a knock on his door. He waits for the door to open. The dog, which has been lying across his feet, stands in anticipation. Because nothing immediately happens, the dog sits down again and sighs.

'William?' he hears. He had expected it to be Don. The fact that it is Fiona makes it all seem much more serious. 'May we come in?'

The door is pushed open. The dog stands, walks to Fiona and sits looking up at her, waiting for instruction. The root of her tail thumps the floor. The woman follows her in and smiles fondly at the dog, then at the boy.

'Hello, Billy,' she says.

*

'What are they saying?' Fiona asks Don. She is standing as close as she can to the lounge door, and listening to the murmur of conversation from Billy's room.

'I don't know, love. Leave them. It won't do any good.'

'You haven't got a clue have you?'

'Me? A clue about what?'

'Exactly.'

'She'll come down and tell us.'

'It's a . . . bloody mess, this whole thing.'

'Don't upset yourself.'

'Oh, for heaven's sake.'

'We've done the right thing by bringing her here. Let's just wait until she's talked to the lad.'

Fiona takes the octagonal plate to the kitchen and scrapes nine uneaten pastries into the silver bin. Don and the dog, which has been ordered downstairs, watch the disposal of the food with similar feelings of bereavement.

'Is that what you hoped, Billy?' the woman asks.

'Don't know.'

'Come on. This is your opportunity to tell me exactly how you're feeling. If you don't tell me, I can't help you, can I? And I'm here to help you.'

'I suppose so.'

'Is that what you've hoped since you came here?'

'When I'm eighteen they can't tell me what to do.'

'That's nearly eight years.'

'I know.'

'And how do you know you'll feel the same in eight years' time?'

'I will.'

'All right, and what if your mother doesn't feel the same?'

'She does.'

'But you can't know that.'

'I can.'

'Billy. I think you're just going to have to accept that . . . that it's unlikely you will be living with your mother again. Don and Fiona have fostered you and may adopt you which means you'll be legally in their care.'

'And when I'm eighteen I can leave and they can't stop me.'

'Your mother is in hospital again.'

Billy nods.

'Is that what you thought?'

Billy nods again.

'It's the right place for her. She needs . . . help.'

'Can I see her?'

'Yes. But not until she comes out.'

'Why didn't you tell me?'

'Because I think it was felt it would be best if you didn't know.'

'Why?'

'. . . I think the general feeling was that we didn't want to worry you.'

'When will she come out?'

'Two weeks perhaps. Perhaps three.'

'So can I see her in three weeks?'

'When the time is right.'

Billy goes to his drawer and brings out his bar of Galaxy chocolate. He breaks off one piece and hands it to the woman.

'Is this your secret supply?' she asks him.

'My mum bought it for me.'

'. . . And is it a never-ending bar?'

'No.'

'Thank you, Billy.'

'S'all right.'

'Do you think it might help you to talk to somebody?'

'About what?'

'About how you're feeling.'

'I talk to you.'

'Yes. But we have people who . . . who are like me and who you could meet – say – every few days and just tell them what's on your mind.'

'Could I talk to you?'

'Well, I . . .'

'Please could it be you?'

'All right, Billy. I'll see what I can do.'

13

Jane has found that if she concentrates hard the buzz in her head goes away. Lying in her hospital bed, her mind roams until she finds herself remembering a day from many years before when she went down to the river to look for him. She focuses her thoughts. The image sharpens. That day the river was low. The warehouses on the far side looked like ugly criminal havens. One of them was painted canary yellow and advertised self-storage. The windows were whited out. A chalky-white line marked the high-water point on the river wall. The mud banks were scattered with litter and patterned with the prints of gulls' feet. She checked her *A–Z* before continuing her journey.

Her destination proved to be a 1930s mansion block. The flagstones of the wide path were as clean as if they had just been laid. They were bordered by beds of pruned roses. The soil was moist and a lush brown. Jane hurried up the path and pushed the front door open. She paused, peering into the hallway that smelt of polish, and then she went in. Having crossed the chequered tiles, she read the names on the vault of letterboxes. She fixed on number 37.

The thick carpet cushioned her tread as she walked along the corridor of light wood doors. To Jane it felt more like a hotel than a block of flats. There was no sound at all from the apartments she passed. She reached number 37, paused and knocked. The door was opened smartly by a middle-aged man in a pressed, short-sleeved white shirt. A pair of sleek glasses with small rectangular frames protruded from the breast pocket of his shirt. His hair was yellowy-grey and he had what Jane considered to be shrewd eyes, though they were sunk deep into wrinkled brown skin. He looked a little like the piano-tuner although he was older and heavier in the jowls. Jane could hear a woman inside the flat talking like a teacher. She seemed to be admonishing somebody but, because she went on and on, Jane realized her voice was coming from the radio.

'Yes?' the man said in the English way which could have been interpreted as businesslike or rude depending on how strong you were feeling.

Jane looked at him blankly.

'Can I help you?' he said more softly, having quickly been mellowed by Jane's looks.

'You look like . . .' She took out the photograph of John.

'I look like what?'

'John.'

'You know my brother?' he said, glancing at the photograph in her hand.

'Yes, oh yes. Is he in?'

There was a moment in which the man tried to understand what the two of them could have had in common. Jane smelt the polish on the wooden panels of the hallway until it was no longer unfamiliar to her. She would only be aware of it again when she took off her coat that evening and caught a draught of it from the fabric. The man said: 'No. I'm afraid he isn't. But you're most welcome to come in.'

He stood back and Jane walked past him and into the flat. The floors were parquet, scarred and sealed with thick wax which made the old wood look orange. The living room was furnished with 1930s furniture. There was an ashtray on a stalk, a squared pile of interior design magazines on the low table, a potted palm, a naked woman cast in bronze, leaping like a stag, a light bulb in her outstretched palms. And, in the bay of the metal-framed window, a black, baby grand piano.

'Please. Sit down.' The man gestured to a two-seater settee which had wooden arms that were curved like vintage-car mudguards. Jane sat primly, her hands in her lap in the way the settee demanded she should sit.

'I should introduce myself. I'm Anthony. As I told you, John's brother.'

'Yes. I know.'

'I'm forgetting my manners. Would you like a coffee or a tea, or . . .?'

'Coffee. Yes. Thank you. No Milk. No sugar.'

'Of course.' Anthony stood and waved vaguely towards the far end of the room. 'Please. Just make yourself at home.'

When Anthony had gone out to the small kitchenette Jane looked around the room for traces of him.

'I don't actually live here,' Anthony called over the grinding of coffee beans. 'This is John and Lucy's place . . . I pop in from time to time and keep an eye on it when they're away. They've gone to stay with her father in Dorset for a few days . . . he hasn't been well.'

Jane caught sight of a photograph in a frame on the mantelpiece. She stood and approached it: Anthony, John and a woman between them. She picked it up and held it in both hands. The woman was a head shorter than Anthony but the same height as John. It had never occurred to her before that John was short, nor had it struck her that Anthony had been particularly tall. It looked like a wedding photograph although the clothes were studiedly casual. The woman was holding a bouquet of wild flowers and wearing a hat which looked like an inverted flower pot. One of the mothers at Billy's school dressed similarly for effect. She thought her baggy jeans and long cardigans and woolly hats gave her a sense of style – but Jane thought they just made her look desperate, like a child wanting to belong. One thing was for sure: she wasn't the hippy she pretended to be. Jane was grateful that at least she had a sense of who she was – even if it was a bit blurry sometimes.

She put the photograph down, crossed over to the piano,

sat at the stool and raised the lid. She laid her fingers on the keys, fully spread, then she exerted a gentle pressure with the first finger of her right hand. A note was born, and lived its brief life before passing away like a fly through a window. Jane looked towards the door and saw Anthony watching her.

'Do you play?' he said. 'I mean is that how you met John?'

'He's a piano-tuner.'

'Amongst other things. I mean what he actually is is a rather good composer, but he has to make a living . . . Do you play did you say?'

'No.' Jane returned her attention to the keyboard.

'I won't keep you a moment.' Anthony darted out of the room again. 'You were telling me how you met,' he called from the kitchen.

'Was I?'

'Yes.'

'I was having my heel mended.'

'I'm sorry?' Anthony's face reappeared around the edge of the door.

'At the heel bar. My shoe broke and I was sitting on a stool . . . and I looked up and saw him watching me. From across the road.'

'I see,' Anthony said, trying to visualize his brother catching sight of Jane. He failed. His face withdrew again.

Jane left the piano stool and drifted to another framed photograph in a cabinet: John and Lucy, alone this time on an exotic terrace overlooking an expensive blue sea. She picked it up then put it down again trying not to feel the jealousy it tried to provoke in her. She opened a drawer and looked inside. Only papers.

Anthony came in a moment later with two tiny cups and a silver coffee pot on a tray. Unembarrassed, Jane closed the drawer. Anthony put one of the cups down onto the low table. Jane came back to the settee and sat down. Anthony took the armchair next to her. Jane crossed her legs. She noticed him noticing her.

'You say you met John when you'd broken your shoe?'

'Yes. I caught my heel in a drain.'

It had been raining and she hadn't been concentrating; usually she concentrates hard when she walks. The heel bar was close by. It looked bright and cheerful in the dull street of shops: a beacon of yellow light like an American diner with three tall stools set against the high counter. A woman was sitting at one of the stools in a damp mac. Three supermarket carrier bags crowded her feet like sleeping dogs. She was massaging a bunion on her right foot through her tights while the neat-looking shoe mender, his back to her, fixed the sole of her leather boot. The woman stared at Jane when she came in and then looked quickly away as if she had found her looks intimidating. She stopped massaging her foot. It was the way she chose to salvage her pride: not being observed massaging her bunion by a girl graced with beauty and youth. But when she did turn away she regretted it because she was now committed to facing the side wall of the shop with its boring cards of shoelaces and shelves of polishes.

Jane had taken the stool at the furthest end of the counter. When the man gave the woman her boot back, he winked at Jane. Jane took off her shoe and put it on the counter. The woman paid the shoe mender then went off, somehow managing to keep her back to Jane throughout the whole manoeuvre. She had trouble opening the door because of her shopping bags but somehow managed to nudge the handle down with her elbow and get out before the shoe mender had reached the door to help her.

'Let's have a look at this then, shall we?' the man said, having returned to the counter and picked up Jane's shoe by its broken heel. He held it at eye height. 'Cost you a fiver. Worth it, though, for a shoe of this quality.' The shoe mender was wearing a leather apron, his hair was greased back like an old-fashioned footballer, and he had a half-smoked cigarette behind his ear.

'All right,' Jane said, as if a fiver was nothing to her.

The man smiled. When he turned to his machine with its levers, belts and wheels he seemed immediately to become a part of it: a metal cockroach man. The shoe bar smelt wholesome and made Jane want to fill her lungs with it – the opposite of butcher's shops which always reeked of decay and bleach.

It was then that she saw a man staring at her from the other side of the road. She wondered for a moment if they had met because his interest in her was so naked. And all the time that she watched him – looking left and right, then dashing through the traffic and rain, his hands deep in the pockets of his mac – she imagined he must have been looking for her for a reason. Perhaps she had dropped her purse and he had picked it up and had been chasing her. That was how determined he seemed. But when he came into the heel bar, earning a nod from the shoe mender who turned briefly from his task, he stood in front of her and didn't seem to know what he wanted to say.

Jane immediately liked the look of him. She was flattered that a youngish, elegant-looking man in linen, sand-coloured trousers, a fashionably crumpled shirt and a nice mac would make a fool of himself for her. But what she liked even more about him was that he'd done something that she knew she was capable of: acting without any consideration of the consequences.

'Do you cut keys?' the man asked the shoe mender. His voice was gentle but clipped and posh.

'Be with you in a mo'.' The shoe mender was used to people trying to rush him and he'd developed a soothing tone of voice which acknowledged the time pressure while assuring the customer he was working as fast as he could.

The man sat at the stool beside Jane's and took out a key ring with three keys on it. He lifted it by its thin fob chain so that the keys hung vertically, then draped them sound-lessly onto the counter. His fingers, Jane noticed, were long and delicate. His nails were beautifully tended, his cuticles bright quarter moons. After laying down his keys, the man leant his elbows on the counter as though he was at a public bar.

After a while he turned his face towards Jane, and she was glad because she had thought he'd lost his nerve. She willed him to speak; she didn't want to be the one who spoke first.

He said: 'You are astonishingly beautiful.' And that was how it had all begun.

'He didn't say that!' the Sugar Plum Fairy said, when Jane told her the story.

'He did.'

'Nobody says that – except on the telly.'

'I swear he did.'

'And you didn't laugh?'

'No. Of course I didn't. Would you?'

'Yes.'

'Well, that's where we're different.'

'But you are beautiful, I suppose,' the Sugar Plum Fairy said, as if it had only just occurred to her. 'And I'm not, so if a boy said that to me he'd probably be pissed and just trying to get into my knickers.'

'And what – I don't mean to pry – what exactly is your relationship with my brother . . .?' Anthony asked. He had put his coffee cup on the table as if it was just another object of beauty.

Jane sipped the bitter coffee, wondering how honest she could be with him. He was not a man who inspired trust, even though he seemed to think he did.

'What I mean to say is . . . do you know Lucy too? I mean are you friends of both of them or . . .?'

'I don't know Lucy.'

'No. I somehow imagined you wouldn't.'

'There's a man I know,' Jane said, not much liking Anthony's sneering tone. 'He's called Patrick.'

'Yes? Patrick is your friend is he?' Anthony had now adopted the tone he employed with children and the mentally deficient.

'He runs a bookshop – Patrick's Books – it's not far from here. And behind his counter he has photographs. Dozens of photographs. He pins them up in his gallery.'

Anthony nodded politely.

'They're all bookmarks, you see? People leave them in books and they sell them to Patrick and he . . . it's a gallery.'

'I'm not entirely sure what this has to do with John.' Anthony smiled to suggest that the reason for his lack of understanding lay entirely with him.

'I bought a book from Patrick. Guy de Maupassant. It was . . .'

'*Pierre et Jean.*'

'How did you know?'

'John re-reads it. Every year. He presses it upon people; insists that they absolutely must read it.'

'And did you?'

'Yes. I found it rather . . . overwrought. Two brothers, a mother fixation, a sum of money willed to one of the brothers from an old family friend which revealed to him, to all the family in fact, that the man he'd considered all his life to be his father, was actually no such thing.' Anthony stood and went to the book shelves. 'And you say you bought this book from Patrick's shop?'

'Yes.'

'. . . And you assumed it to be John's copy. Is that right?'

'It had his photograph in it. But it was torn in half. He was in the park. By the temple.'

Anthony came over to her and sat down beside her. 'Let me just get this straight, there's something here that . . . You say that you know John?'

'Yes. I've told you that.'

'And you also say that you went to a second-hand bookshop – and you bought a copy of *Pierre et Jean* which had his photograph in it . . . is that what you're saying?'

Jane nodded.

'Well, isn't that the most remarkable coincidence? I mean I'm not for one moment doubting what you're telling me. Don't for a second think that. But, nonetheless, you have to admit that . . .'

'I sold it to him. To Patrick.'

Anthony nodded slowly.

'And then I bought it back again.'

'. . . OK.'

'Does that sound strange?'

'Well, not in the sense that . . . You sold a bookseller the copy of *Pierre et Jean* that John had given you, leaving a photograph of him inside it – and then you bought it back from him.'

'Yes. That's what I did.'

'And when you bought it back it still had the photograph of John in it that you had used as a bookmark.'

'Yes. But I'd sold it to him before. Twice. And then I'd bought it back again.'

'Why?'

'Because I had to. Because . . . Could I have some milk, please?' Jane held out her cup of coffee.

'I'm sorry. I thought you asked for it black.'

'No. Milk no sugar.'

'Of course.'

As soon as he left the room Jane stood, took one more look around and let herself silently out.

'Wait, please! Wait!' Anthony called as she reached the lift, but the doors closed as he ran towards her.

Jane hurried out at the ground floor. When she heard footsteps dashing down the stairs she tensed. She saw a door to a cleaners' cupboard beside the letter box vault. She went inside and pulled the door to. Through the crack she watched Anthony dash out of the building.

All of this happened a number of her yesterdays ago but she is remembering it today, in the hospital ward, as she lies alone. Of course it had been long before John disappeared, before he died, before the light of him went out.

14

When the Sugar Plum Fairy is in the hospital at the same time as Jane they spend most of their time together. If she is not, it rarely takes Jane long to find somebody to talk to. Today she is sitting with a sixty-three-year-old woman whose skin has become parched and ingrained with nicotine stains after a long career of heavy smoking. The woman's eyes are dull; her limbs shake when she is not fully occupied with her knitting.

'. . . like in the war,' the woman says, concluding a long rambling anecdote. Jane listens to her needles clicking like cat's teeth and watches her head bobbing up and down. The woman has been talking for some time. Jane has made only an occasional contribution just to remind herself that she is still capable of speech.

After a brief pause the woman goes on: '. . . an' him an'

everything. Everything. That's what it . . . Like the war. An'. An'. An'. An' I know it didn't mean anything to him, jus'. Jus'. What he said an' all.'

'What's his name?'

'Names.'

'His names then. What are his names?'

'Charlie. My Charlie. Charlie Charles.' The old woman laughs. 'He's coming up here tonight. That's what – anyway – anyway, he says he might, how d'you expect me to . . . only you'd best not tickle him because he don't like that. He might jus' give you a right good old slap.'

'Your husband?'

'Charlie Charles. Fancy calling a boy that. His father was a cruel man. Worked on the railways. He went out at all hours to . . . where's my glasses?'

'On your head.'

'You're a fine one to . . . he's got a lovely voice: Vibriato. You should hear him when he gets going.'

'What does he sing?'

'Anything you ask him: "Mona Lisa", "My Way", some of the pop songs.'

Jane shifts in her chair. She wants a bath but she has already had three today and they won't let her have the plug again. The last time she was in there they got a pass key and a butch nurse came in and pulled the plug out of the hole without asking her. When the water was gone, Jane sat in the bath shivering, her knees up to her chest. The woman draped a large towel around her shoulders. Jane threw it off petulantly and continued to shiver. The woman put it on her again and waited while she dried herself. As Jane was dressing the woman took out a half-smoked, untipped cigarette from her pocket, straightened it and lit it. She looked towards the door of the bathroom then kicked it shut with the toe of her trainer because a male cleaner was watching.

'Why do you keep coming in here?' the woman asked her.

'Because I like to stay clean.'

'Is that the only reason?'

'No.'

'So what's the other reason?'

'I'm not telling you.'

'Suit yourself.' The woman pinched a fleck of tobacco from her lower lip. Jane liked her because she didn't pretend the job was any more important than it was. She knew she was just a minder for people who were a bit mad, nothing more. She had no hand in curing them but it was down to her that they didn't escape or hang themselves with their tights or cut themselves with knives they stole from the canteen. She also had to make sure none of them fell asleep against the radiators and burned their faces.

'All right. I'll tell you if you want,' Jane said.

'I'm not fussed.'

'Sometimes I can talk to him in here.'

'Who?'

'John.'

'And what does this John say to you?'

'He tells me everything is going to be all right.'

'And you believe him?'

'Yes. Because everything always is all right. Eventually. At least for a while.'

'I suppose that's true enough.'

15

'Son?' Don says, and waits for the boy to answer. Unlike his wife, Don will not enter Billy's room without permission. The door is pushed to but not closed.

'Son?' he tries again. Billy allows him this indulgence. Fiona has a more difficult role to play – the position of his mother having already been taken.

'I've got your grub . . . William?' He waits, and then leans down and puts the tray on the landing. 'I've put your food on the landing . . . Righty ho, then. I'll leave you to get on with it.'

Don goes to the top of the stairs where he pauses for a moment in anticipation of Billy opening the door. But the door does not open. When he is three steps down he is surprised to hear that it does.

'I want to see her,' Billy says. Don cannot turn around on

the narrow staircase so he backs up to the landing. The sight of the boy shocks him. He knows he should be used to it by now but the circles beneath his eyes, which seem to shine far too brightly, and the thinness of the child's face remind him of his own mother shortly before her death. But there is apparently nothing physically wrong with Billy. The doctor had assured them of this: that he was thin, not under-nourished. Then he reiterated it: 'Nothing *physically* wrong,' and Fiona afterwards said he might as well have nudged them in the ribs or winked.

Don and Billy face each other across the tray. On the white dinner plate is a perfect pyramid of mashed potato; four pork sausages are lying around the base. Fiona had shaped the potato with a warm, long-bladed knife. Although she had not intended to, she'd become so fixated by making the pyramid perfect that it had taken her ten minutes. When she had completed it to her satisfaction the meal was cold so she had warmed it up in the microwave. When Don had taken the tray from her she had set about cleaning the condensation from the inside of the microwave with a kitchen towel. The only thing she liked more than a pristine kitchen was one which needed a little cleaning.

'Who do you want to see, William?' Don asks.

'The social-work lady. She said I could talk to her.'

'I don't know.'

'She said I could.'

Don sighs. He feels an old anxiety provoked by his previous dealings with the health services: an anxiety of unentitlement. Although he knows he has every right to use a GP or the hospitals, deep down he feels that others have a much greater claim on them than he does. But, faced with the boy's anguished face, he realizes he should have acted sooner and would have done, had Fiona not talked him out of it. After the support worker's last visit, his wife had decided to put a brave face on it and told her friend at Pilates that they were going to weather the storm and go through with the adoption. The boy was going through a difficult phase, but he'd be all right when he realized what kind of life he could have with them.

'I'll call her first thing tomorrow.' Don says. Already he is tense from the row this will provoke.

Billy picks up the tray.

'Lad . . .?'

'What?'

'You can talk to me you know.'

'William!' they both hear from the lounge.

'I know,' Billy says.

'William,' Fiona calls. 'Are you getting on with that meal?'

'Yes,' Billy calls as if it pains him to raise his voice. They wait but Fiona is satisfied.

'I mean we could go out – do something. Go to a . . . football match,' Don says. 'Blokes' outing. Would you like that?'

'All right.'

'Anyway, you get on with that while it's still warm.'

'OK.'

'But don't forget.'

'No. You'll call the lady?'

'Promise.'

'Don!' they hear from the lounge. 'Don, what are you doing up there?'

Don smiles and, for the first time in as long as he can remember, Billy smiles back.

16

This time, when Jane is released from the hospital, Alf is waiting in the reception to collect her.

'How did you know I was coming out?' she asks him. The reception is the brightest and cleanest area of the hospital complex. It is the only place in which there are potted plants.

'They told me. It's all right. I used my bus pass.' Alf makes the final statement towards the receptionist and Jane realizes they must have been chatting together while he was waiting for her. Perhaps, beyond Alf's mode of transport, they had been discussing her. She decides to let it pass.

'You look smart, Alf,' she says.

'Well, I thought I'd make an effort – on account of it being you.' Alf picks up Jane's small suitcase and leads off.

'Thank you.'

The front doors slide open by magic as they approach them. Outside, as she steps from the kerb onto the road, Jane feels unsteady on her feet and reaches for Alf's arm. The world is moving fast. By the time they have reached the bus stop she has begun to get used to the pace of it again. She is aware from the look on Alf's face that she must look different.

'I'm all right,' she assures him.

'It's a shame, that's all.'

'What is?'

'You. Your situation. It doesn't seem right. I feel sorry for you.'

'There's no need.'

'I know. That's why I do.'

When the bus arrives, Alf leads the way upstairs. It pulls off when Jane is halfway up. This paralyses her with fright and she clings onto the silver rail until her knuckles turn white. Alf comes back down the stairs and tries to help her up but she won't let go. Finally he has to call to the driver to pull over, and only then does Jane allow him to lead her downstairs to the lower deck. Everybody watches her as she walks along the aisle to the back seat, which is the only one free. Alf follows in her wake, smiling at the staring people to placate them.

'I don't want to go straight home,' Jane says, looking out of the bus window when they are safely seated. Each time the bus stops the raindrops judder; an inverted street scene is captured in each tiny globe.

'Where do you want to go then, love?' Alf sits in his seat, straight backed. Jane has always admired Alf for his pride.

'I don't know.'

'Well I've got no plans to speak of. I'm happy to follow instructions.'

'I'd like to go to the zoo.'

'The zoo?'

'I don't want to put you out.'

'No. The zoo. That's all right. I'd be happy to spend a couple of hours there.'

'Thank you,' Jane says and when she kisses Alf on the cheek she can smell that he has been drinking.

While they are standing at the waist-high wall watching the penguins, Jane is overwhelmed by such a profound sadness that she can't hold back her tears. Alf reaches out and touches her arm. He looks over his shoulder; he doesn't want it to look like he has caused her misery. What has upset Jane is the cheerless, concrete world in which they are imprisoned. The floor of the pool has been painted a duck-egg blue, but all the penguins are standing on the grey terraces behind it, peering accusingly in Jane's direction. She feels that they are imploring her to put them out of their misery.

'Come on, love. Let's get you inside,' Alf says and leads her gently away towards the café. She feels as though she has momentarily forgotten how to walk but, after she has taken the first few steps with Alf's arm around her shoulders, the next few come more easily and she remembers again.

When Hackett and her mother left her that day, only her mother walked with her to the front door of the Victorian house. The door looked very tall; taller and wider than any door Jane thought she had ever seen. Above it was a stained glass window. A woman answered the bell, drying her hands on a tea towel. She had flour on her sleeve and on her right cheek. Jane's mother shook her cold hand by making a brief clasp of her fingers. The woman said, 'So this is young Jane, is it?' And Jane had not replied. In that moment, the woman seemed to have made up her mind about her: she needed to be sorted out, taken in hand, taught some manners and taught her place. Jane heard the woman use all these phrases in the days and months to come. She resisted for as long as she could; after all, for all their faults, her mother and Hackett had never made her feel as if she had any shortcomings. But soon she learned that for her life to have any comfort and peace, she had to learn like a dog how to behave in the woman's house. It didn't help that she was also fostering a brother and sister, who, although they were younger than Jane, were much wilier. They were also safer because they lived in a world where only they knew the rules and the language, and strangers like Jane didn't belong.

The zoo café is warm, tall as a barn, and smells of microwaved pies. A prim elderly couple are the only other customers. They are both wearing their coats and scarves.

The man has a bag of fruit at his feet for the chimpanzees. They cradle cups of tea in the same way. They are sitting side by side, watching as Alf leads Jane to a seat by the window. Outside, there is a small children's play area which is empty.

'It'll take a while, I should think,' Alf says. 'To get yourself back to normal.'

'Yes,' Jane agrees. 'It usually does.'

'I'm trying to think what's been going on since you've been . . . since you've not been there.'

'How's Maude?'

'Well, she's getting some gyp from her leg. Other than that Maude's Maude.'

'Did somebody turn my fridge off and leave it open?'

'I don't know, love. I expect so. Maude went in and said she'd sorted everything out so I should think she'll have done all that kind of thing.'

'Only it goes mouldy if you don't leave the door open.'

'I can't say but I expect Maude's seen to it.'

'And how's Carey?'

'I think he had some bother with The Boy. There was some palaver one Saturday night. Maude said she was going to call the police, but it all quietened down again.'

'Why are they staring at us?'

'What?'

'Them. Why are they staring?'

Alf smiles towards the old couple. But they continue to stare.

'Fuck off!' Jane shouts.

They stop staring. The woman behind the counter lifts the flap and strides across the room towards Jane.

'Aye, aye. That's done it,' Alf says, draining his tea.

'I'm going to have to ask you to leave,' the woman says, folding her arms as she reaches them.

'They were staring,' Jane tells her.

'There's no excuse for that kind of language.'

'Tell them off then. You tell me off for swearing, why don't you tell them off for being rude?'

'I've asked you to leave. I won't ask you again.'

'Or what?'

'It's all right, we're going,' Alf says.

'You should be ashamed of yourself,' Jane says. 'Keeping those poor penguins in that horrible place.'

'We have experts here. It's not cruel. You should read the leaflet.'

'I don't need a leaflet to tell me that those birds are sad.'

'Birds don't get sad. It's not in their nature.'

'And how would you know?'

'I'd know better than you I should think. I make it my business to know.'

'All God's creatures get sad.'

'Come on, love.' Alf stands and pats down his pockets out of habit.

'How do you know?' Jane challenges the woman again.

'I see them every day, so I expect I'm more qualified to hold an opinion than you are. Anyway, we've got a canary indoors.'

'Canaries aren't penguins.'

'We taught our canary to sing – so I expect I've got some expertise in that field. He sings along to *Steve Wright in the afternoon*.'

'If I saw them every day I'd do something about it.'

'I'm not going to say this again. Just go.' The woman directs the next appeal to Alf. 'Take her away. We don't tolerate that kind of behaviour here.'

'It's all right,' Alf says. 'We're leaving.'

'You never stand up for me,' Jane accuses him.

'I think you're quite capable of doing that for yourself aren't you?' Alf leads the way to the door, indifferent as to whether or not Jane follows him.

Standing, Jane drains her teacup. She hands the empty cup to the woman, and then crosses the room to the old couple.

'I'm sorry,' she says when she reaches them. The woman nods but holds the hate on her face. The man is nervous of offering any response.

'Only I've been in hospital. It's my head that's broken – and it's not quite fixed yet. So I'm sorry. But when you . . . when you're not right you can annoy people. And they think you're a bad person – but if you got cancer and they cut bits out of you, and you didn't get better, people would feel sorry for you – but when your head gets broken it's all messy inside and you say things you wouldn't normally . . . But you were staring at me. And you can still fuck off.'

*

'Shouldnthavesaiditshouldnthavesaiditshouldnthavesaidit',
Jane repeats again and again as she walks around her flat,
trailing her fingers behind her through the dust on every
surface – a thick white powder that seems to have come
down from the ceiling. There's so much of it that she looks
up to see whether a trap door has opened and somebody has
tipped a wheelbarrow of it down on top of her.

She closes the fridge door and turns it on at the plug. The
dwarf inside it begins to whistle. She opens the valve on the
radiator, holds her hand against it and feels the heat flood-
ing in. After five minutes, the unfamiliar smell of the place
has become familiar. She sits on the bed and wonders what
her life used to be for. If she didn't have the illness to recover
from sometimes she wonders what her purpose would be.
Apart from Billy. Billy! Remembering her son she dashes to
the calendar, tears off a sheet of used-up days and sees the
date that has been circled for their meeting. The date means
nothing to her. She has lost all track of time.

Jane takes the calendar from the wall, dashes down the
corridor and knocks on Alf's door. When he answers she asks
him what date it is. He has to fetch his morning paper and
then find his glasses before he can tell her. Deep down she
already knows that she has missed her meeting with Billy.

Jane lies on her bed and the day goes along without her. She
tries to sleep but she cannot. She rolls over and buries her
face in the pillow. It smells unfamiliar. Somebody has been
sleeping in her bed. Then she realizes it is the smell of her

own best perfume still clinging to the fabric after four weeks' absence. She feels like a different woman now. Those four weeks feel like forty years.

17

Billy lies on the bed face down and pulls a pillow tight around his ears. When he lifts it again he can hear the sound of the argument from the living room below. Very little happens in Fiona and Don's house which surprises him; he feels almost proud that they have managed to rouse themselves sufficiently to engage in a proper argument. But because they haven't done it before they don't really know the rules, so everything is being employed in the verbal assault. Fiona is using the 'bad, bad words' she will not allow Billy to say. She is shrill and vicious; for a few minutes Don's dead mother has been the target, her fire then drifts off harmlessly towards the house, the neighbourhood, the lack of decent shops, before she finds her range again, fixing on Don himself: his clumsiness, his lack of ambition, his ineptness in company and what passes for his sexual technique.

When she pauses for breath, her breath catching in her throat, Don's anger is allowed tentative expression. His is delivered more economically: a series of short verbal blows. He counters Fiona by talking about the amount of his money she spends on clothes, the fact that many women would be satisfied with the life she has and which he provides for her. But then he makes the mistake of pausing. Even in the heat of their anger Don remains deferential. And it is at this point that Fiona returns briefly to Don's inability to satisfy her sexual appetites, using this as a springboard into the infertility treatment and, inevitably, on to the root cause of the disagreement: William himself, or 'that boy', as Fiona chooses to call him.

'That . . . boy. He's no more than an animal: he's sly, he's dirty, he doesn't give a damn about us. In fact I'm sure that if we were knocked down by a bus tomorrow, he wouldn't care. In fact. In fact I'm sure he'd be glad.'

'Now you're talking rubbish,' Don says.

'What he needs is a good hiding. We've, you've, been too soft on him. All that nonsense we've had to listen to from Miss Hoity-Toity in her little blouses coming here telling us how best to cope with . . . buy the child a dog, take him out, give him space, don't judge him too hard. Well, what about me! What about my floor with dog hairs all over it. What about me not being able to take the little bastard out on the street for fear he's going to embarrass me or run off. When did she ever give a moment's thought to that?'

Billy, by now, has moved silently from his room to the

landing where he is sitting at the top of the stairs. The dog, not being allowed up (although exceptions are occasionally made), is standing at the bottom. The focus of her attention, signalled by the direction of her nose, shifts from Billy to the living room where the row is taking place. She can't quite decide which has more of a bearing on her next walk or bowl of food.

'. . . ever think about yourself. That's all. That's all you've ever done. Think about yourself,' Don says.

'That's what you think is it? Is it Don? Is this cards-on-the-table-time? Because if it is, I promise you this. If you think I'm cooking one more meal for you when you get back in the house at twenty-five to bloody seven at night you're mistaken. And if you think I'm washing any more of your stinking clothes, then think again. In fact don't think again. Go away. Go and live somewhere else.'

'You don't mean that . . .'

'Yes. Yes I do and I'll tell you what. You come back here in four weeks' time and you'll see a change in that boy. Believe me, he will not know what's hit him. I'll sit with him and I'll force that food down his throat – so help me God – and I'll make him respect me. And if you think – or he thinks I'm opening my door to that bitch of a so-called support worker one more time then you're both mistaken. The sooner that boy learns that . . . mess of a mother is not coming to fetch him back the better, the better for all of us – and then maybe we can all move on . . .'

Billy moves wearily back into his room and closes the

door. The row has paused. He can hear the rumble of Don's voice through the floor, but it's more measured; opinions are being exchanged, a peace treaty written up. He sits on his bed and looks out of the window towards the telegraph pole and the streetlight that looks like a giraffe's head against the dusk. Billy stands again, goes to his drawer and takes out the bar of Galaxy his mother had given him. There are two pieces left. He had intended to save them until the social-work woman came to talk to him, but now it seemed she wouldn't be coming, which meant that the life-line to his mother had been cut. His plan was of no use to him now.

This is what he was going to do: he was going to take some money with him when the woman drove him to meet his mother. They would meet for their carefully measured hour and a half in a café in the shopping centre. About half an hour in, when everybody was relaxed and the woman had pulled her chair back a bit from the table, he was going to get out his money. Then, as if he'd forgotten, he was going to say something like – 'I wanted to buy Mum some choco-late. I've saved up for it.' The woman would then, he hoped, volunteer to go and get some. She knew how important chocolate was to the two of them. This was the tricky moment because she didn't usually leave them on their own. But he reckoned she trusted him enough not to let her down. And as soon as the woman was out of sight he was going to grab his mother's hand and they were going to run away as fast as they could. A good plan. But it was of no use now.

*

He puts both pieces of chocolate into his mouth, crunches them quickly to a pulp and then swallows them without tasting them. They were safe now, inside him. Nobody could have the one thing he had that was left of her.

He had opened the bar so carefully that he had managed to remove the chocolate without tearing the paper wrapper. He decided that he would keep it safe inside his *Guinness Book of World Records*. So he gently flattened the wrapper out onto his desk and peeled off the gold foil. It came away easily, as if somebody had taken it off before. And it was then, with the foil off, that he found the note in the childlike hand, written in biro on the inside of the wrapper. It said: 'I love you, Billy. You know that, soldier. Mummy.' And there were seven kisses. But more important than those, much more important, was that she had written an address underneath. Billy's surge of hope was immediately tempered by the sobering realization that he had had the chocolate for six months. More than six months. She would have assumed he would have eaten it the moment he got home and would have been waiting for him to turn up ever since then. Perhaps she had decided he didn't want to go back to her. Perhaps that was why she had made herself ill again.

The anxiety provoked by this fear floods Billy's stomach and squeezes his heart so tight that he feels he can't catch his breath. There was one hope: that she thought he hadn't gone to find her because he hadn't seen the address.

He hears a sound from the hallway: his cutlery is being

put onto the plate and the tray is being picked up. He reaches for the wrapper and pushes it under his pillow. He knows that if it is Fiona she won't bother to come in. If it is Don, he will knock and offer some weak words of conciliation. He concludes it is Fiona because he immediately hears footsteps on the stairs. When she gets to the bottom he hears her telling the dog to get out of the way.

Billy looks out at the night which has just fallen and the giraffe's head is lit up orange. He has new plans to make now and this time nobody is going to spoil them. Everything will be all right soon.

18

'Hello, love,' Patrick says as Jane comes into the shop and, even in her misery, she is grateful that he seems so happy to see her. Patrick has changed in the time she has been away. He looks less tired around the eyes and a weight seems to have been lifted from his shoulders.

'I've missed you,' he says, but she can see that he's wary of her as she approaches the desk. Something of her ordeal must still be showing in her face despite the make-up. He looks as though he's preparing to spring back out of her range should she decide to lash out at him.

'Cuppa?' he tries, reaching below the counter to switch on the kettle. Jane has drifted towards the desk and stands looking at Patrick's photo-gallery.

'I've been in hospital,' Jane says, finally.

'You should have let me know. I'd have come in to see

you.' Patrick refuses to let Jane's sombre tone infect him. 'I could have brought you some grapes and sat there eating them and we could have pretended to be an old married couple by not saying anything.'

'I wasn't allowed visitors.'

'No?'

'Only at the end.'

'Well that sounds more like prison to me.'

'It is. But it's for your own good.'

'But you're much better now, Jane. I can see that.'

'Can you?'

'Oh, yes.'

'What can you see?'

'I can see . . . I can see a young woman who's been in a long, dark tunnel and she's just coming out the other end.'

The kettle has boiled; Patrick feels the familiar warm steam around his groin. He reaches down, glad of the excuse to avert his eyes from the pain he can see in Jane's face. He pours the water into Jane's mug and drops in a tea-bag. When he hands the mug to Jane she wraps her palms around it.

'I'm all . . .' she says, and then stops.

'You're all what?'

'At sea. Is that how it looks to you?'

'I'd say that I could see something of that, yes.'

'I don't know what to do.'

'About . . .?'

'Billy.'

'Ah. Billy. This is your boy, isn't it?'

'My boy, yes.'

'Well sit yourself down, Jane, and tell me all about it.'

Patrick removes a pile of paperbacks from a wooden chair, dusts it down and invites Jane to sit. She eyes the flimsy chair, decides to trust it, and she sits. For the next half hour she tells Patrick about Billy and although he offers no solutions, she is grateful to have somebody listen to her without making any judgements about her state of mind. And even when she changes tack Patrick keeps up with her.

'. . . It was about his mother, really. When the brother learned that the man he thought was his father wasn't, it changed everything for him,' she says.

'You're talking about *Pierre et Jean*?'

'It changed how he felt about his mother. This perfect woman who he adored wasn't perfect any more. She wasn't just his mother any more, she was a woman who was capable of a great love – but it wasn't love of him, it was love of a man. He lost her then. Suddenly, when he found out about that, then he lost her.'

'Boys and their mothers, eh?'

'He died because of me. John did. He died because of me. But it was her fault. She was the one who really killed him. She killed his spirit. That's worse.'

'It's a long time ago, Jane. Ten years since you were together? Longer?'

'That's no time at all.'

When she leaves the shop she feels she ought to repay

Patrick in some way but she can't think of anything she could offer him that he'd want. He seemed grateful, however, that she'd finally asked him how he was because he told her that Fergal had agreed to invest some more money in the shop. They'd made up and now they were back together and he was happy about that. Their plan was to turn the place into a coffee shop, and now they were discussing whether Patrick should sell books upstairs like they do in Dublin. At the end he told her again that he and Fergal were close and Jane wondered if he had said it to warn her off.

'I hope you do stay here,' Jane says as she reaches the door.

'Well, I might.'

'But for you. I hope you do for you and not just for me.'

'Thank you, Jane. That's a nice thought.'

Jane carries the warmth of Patrick's care with her from the shop. She wears it like a scarf, like the way she wore his care in the two months they had together. Two months to the day from the moment they met in the heel bar to the time he said goodbye for the last time. He had tried to say it before but he hadn't meant it. This goodbye was the worst because when he left her crying, she realized that all the men she had known seemed to belong to somebody else – and she knew it had all begun with Hackett. Fathers were supposed to allow daughters to be pretend-wives so they could learn how to be proper ones, but Hackett had mixed her up with all the games he played with her. There was unfinished business with Hackett. Jane had begun to understand that perhaps the route to her peace of mind lay with seeing him again and telling him exactly what he had done to her. But it had been nearly twenty years since she had seen her parents. They had sent birthday cards dutifully each year but, after the first three years, hadn't managed to write her a letter. They knew where she was. She knew where they were and that was fine. Just fine.

After the last goodbye with him, she had gone around to his flat and met his brother and then she had run away. But she couldn't stay away. That was the trouble. She just couldn't stay. But she was young, only seventeen, and she'd been through a lot. How was she supposed to know how to behave when a man showed her a bit of affection?

'You sound like me,' the Sugar Plum Fairy said one day when they were talking together about their lives. It was high summer. The heat had made them lethargic. They had been sitting on fold-up chairs under a tree in the hospital grounds pretending to be film stars at Cannes. They were drinking orange squash through stripy drinking straws and imagining that they had their backs to the beach because only common people sat staring at the sea. A man was cutting the grass on a sit-down mower and when he was close by the noise of it was so loud they couldn't hear themselves talk. When the mower was out of earshot Jane could hear bird-song; she was only half concentrating on what the Sugar Plum Fairy was saying to her. The cut grass, which made a fine mist in the air, commanded her attention.

'I think I might get some sun.' The Sugar Plum Fairy was tired of having to make all the conversation. 'Unzip me will you,' she said, turning away and offering her broad back to Jane who pulled down the zip on her pink, long-sleeved dress. The Sugar Plum Fairy shrugged out of the top half of it. Underneath she was wearing a ragged, old, pink bra, but Jane was more interested in the cuts on her arms. Some were new red weals, some were old and crusted with dark brown blood. She could make out two words: 'HELP' and 'ME'. They had been carved into the flesh above her wrist.

The Sugar Plum Fairy lay down on the grass and shuffled until she found a comfortable position. 'Sometimes when I'm in here I feel like a newspaper left on a bus,' she said. 'Like I've been passed from hand to hand and read by lots of people in a hurry to be on their way somewhere, then just left on a seat for somebody else to pick up.'

Jane couldn't tear her eyes away from the scars on her arms and the Sugar Plum Fairy sensed her looking. 'I know,' she said. 'It's hard to understand the first time you see it but it's not as bad as it looks.'

'Why?' Jane said.

'Because I can't . . .' but the rest of the explanation was lost under the sound of the lawnmower. By the time it had gone the Sugar Plum Fairy had fallen silent.

Jane had never contemplated cutting herself, but she would have welcomed any distraction from the continuing pain of losing him.

Jane walks away from Patrick's shop and when she hears a car behind her she remembers the conversation she had with the Sugar Plum Fairy that hot afternoon. If she threw herself under it now maybe the pain would all go away. She has nothing left: Billy is gone, she has no real friends and little money. All she has is memories and, somewhere inside her, anger. Anger. She feels it seeping up like the heat in the radiator. It gives her strength and with that strength comes an idea: if she can't give anybody her love, why not give them some of her hate?

Where did *he* live? Come on Jane, try to remember. Where did she visit, that afternoon so long ago, when she walked down to the river and then met his brother and he made her coffee and she ran away? A mansion block. Number 37 – a door down a long corridor with a thick carpet. It was a nice room with expensive antiques. Of course it would all be hers now, Lucy's. Jane hadn't made a fuss before because she'd loved him and she hadn't wanted to make his life difficult. But now he was dead so it didn't matter.

She would go tomorrow to see Lucy. It was time they met.

19

Is this how love feels? Fiona wonders as she looks down at the empty bed. Is this what I have been missing out on all along? Certainly she had never felt this for any man – and she had had great hopes for the one she allowed to pick her up in the library one damp afternoon. She judged him to have been fifteen years older than she was; his age had rendered him unthreatening but had promised wisdom and expertise. As he had driven them back to his bungalow in silence, Fiona had laid her hand in his lap. When they had parked on his drive and he had led the way in through the front door – turned off the alarm, stroked the cat which had pushed its neck against his calf, opened the hallway window to get rid of the smell of the litter tray – only then had he offered to take her coat. He had hung it with old-fashioned care on a brass hook beside the lavatory door. The door was ajar and inside she could see a pink washbasin shaped like a huge shell, gold taps and a crimson carpet. His was the only other coat hanging on the pegs. The neck of it, she now saw, was waxy with grease. A brown scarf occupied another hook.

After he had hung up her coat he had offered her a cup of tea. This is my grand passion, she thought, and my putative lover is offering me a choice of Earl Grey or Typhoo. He even has a pot on a tile-stand and a knitted cosy – clearly he's not a man to rush things or take second best. She accepted the drink because events were in motion and she was enjoying relinquishing control and took a seat in the clean kitchen where one plate, one teaspoon, one knife and one egg cup were sitting on the shining drainer.

Fiona watched as the man made the tea fastidiously, and wondered whether he would exhibit the same care when he made love to her. It was at that point she came to her senses and told him she was leaving. He didn't press her, indeed he offered to drive her back to the library but she told him to call her a taxi; this was the first time she had allowed an edge into her voice. In the fifteen minutes it took to arrive they managed to hold a reasonably civilized conversation, so civilized that it ranged from the yellow-jacketed crime books he had chosen from the library, his former profession of loss-adjuster, his enthusiasm for but limited ability in the kitchen to his passion for the garden. She could see, Fiona said, from the perfect lawn that he knew what he was doing in the garden. But then the conversation had stopped; the absurdity had closed it down. They could not talk about the future because there wasn't one. They had no interest in each other's pasts. And the present was just them; an unsatisfied man and an unsatisfied woman sitting, tense, in the living room of a bungalow waiting for a taxi to arrive.

So is this how love feels? Fiona wonders as she looks down at Billy's bed which has been lain on but not slept in. Perhaps to feel love there must be a fear of loss, so that at the root of love is the fear of being alone. There have been so many times when she has wanted to be somebody else. No. Not somebody else. To be herself. But she's got so used to playing a role that the mask she wears has burned into her face. Perhaps she should have a chemical peel like the woman she saw on the TV make-over show. She would look grotesque for a few weeks, like a burns victim, but perhaps afterwards her real face would emerge and he would love her. They would all love her, and she would no longer need to chide them or bait them into empty declarations of affection.

Did they not understand her? How could they when she barely understood herself. How could she have shown she loved him when he could have walked away from them when he reached eighteen? How could any woman invest that mother-part of herself in a creature that was going to leave in a few years' time and take it away with them? It wasn't fair. It wasn't going to happen. Safer to pretend that the creature hadn't touched you; safer to push him away by doing all the things you knew he hated. Make him call you

'Mum'. Make him hold you tight when you knew it repulsed him. Make him tell you he loved you when you knew it was a statement he could only make with honesty to one woman. And even then she had pressed him until he said it, and she had frightened him with her rage when she pulled his hand from behind his back and made him uncross his fingers. But he wouldn't be humiliated. You could see a great strength in his eyes which would protect him and wouldn't allow him to be defeated by anyone.

Fiona pulls open the curtains to reveal the 2 a.m. street bathed in orange. She has never really needed books or films or TV, the world has always seemed so full of symbols to her. A street after midnight: curtains drawn in all the houses for as far as she can see, a cat slinking, low-shouldered, across the street, a bin bag scored open by a fox, empty cans of cat food scattered in the gutter with ugly serrated tongues, and the long, bobbing shadow made by a streetlight thrown behind a distant, distant boy walking away.

So that was why Fiona had woken. She had been catapult-ed from sleep with such velocity that the moment she opened her eyes she knew something had happened. She had looked across at Don, but the soft purr of his snores allayed her first fear. He wouldn't dare die first and leave her on her own. It came as a shock to her that her second fear was for the creature in the front bedroom. And it wasn't even shame or hurt pride. No. She wasn't afraid of what people would say because he had gone; she was afraid for him, for his safety. Would Don ever understand that, after the argument they had had? Of course he would pretend an understanding but deep down he was always defeated by her contradictions.

Don stirred as she went through his pockets looking for his car keys: 'Man . . . said. Ship, nothing. Don't tell me,' he murmured, 'don't tell me!' Then he had ground his teeth and slipped back into his dream of being a river pilot on a rusty steamboat through the Congo. Fiona took his keys and his wallet and went soundlessly down the stairs, avoiding the third tread which she knew would creak. She covered her nightdress with a thin raincoat, tied the belt, and pushed her feet into William's training shoes. She wondered why he had left them behind. When she found the receipt inside the left one, she realized he hadn't even worn them. But she didn't have time to dwell on this as she went out of the house.

The chill of the night reached out and took her ankles and then crept all the way up her legs until the warmth of her coat pushed it back again. The car-door lock was stiff. She was afraid it was frozen, but she remembered Don telling her you had to pull the key out a little way because there was something wrong with the cylinder. She turned the key, opened the door and the weak interior light washed over her as she slid behind the wheel and onto the cold fabric of the seat. It had been so long since she had driven that she wondered whether she would remember how to do it. Her feet were too far away from the pedals. She couldn't possibly work them from that distance. Then she remembered the bar beneath the seat and reached between her legs for it. It was freezing cold but it lifted easily and she shuffled the seat forward until her right foot found its place on the accelerator and her left rested on the clutch. She let the bar go. Something clicked and the seat locked into place. She looked up into the rear-view mirror but all she could see was the back seat. She angled the mirror down and caught sight of her tired eyes, then up, until she could see the grey road behind her.

When she turned the key the dashboard illuminated with orange and red symbols of warning and reassurance. Don would have explained to her what they meant. He enjoyed showing her that he had mastery of some things even if he didn't have mastery of her. The engine was quiet and she wondered if it had started, but when she pushed the accelerator it shrieked in protest. She decided not to turn on the lights until she had reversed out of the drive and into the road, so she looked over her right shoulder, released the handbrake and the car rolled backwards.

When she let out the clutch and pressed the accelerator she remembered how much she enjoyed driving and how much bigger cars always felt when you were behind the wheel. Her father had bought her her first car, a Mini. The Mini had led her to Don because he had helped her when she couldn't get it started in a pub car park. Her parents had immediately taken to Don; he had charmed her mother because he was so polite and well-turned-out and capable. Fiona had been glad because, for the first time in her life, she felt she had done something right. She couldn't possibly have refused him when, four months after they met, he asked her to marry him. Her only qualm was when she met his mother and she saw the look of naked hate she gave her when Don's back was turned.

She drives slowly along the street, staying in second gear. She had seen William heading towards the shops and assumed he would look for somewhere to sleep until daylight and then move on when the sight of a boy on the street would excite no interest. He would, however, know that the police would be looking for him so perhaps he would get as far away as he could on foot.

Fiona draws up beside the gate of the urban wood before the shops. It is nothing more than two acres of blighted trees and dog-shit-fouled paths; this is all that remains of the forest in which the suburb had taken root. At the centre of the wood is a lake into which black water pours from a mighty, fenced-in weir. At the south end of the lake it drains away, tamed, into the gaping mouth of a subterranean culvert. There are five paths out of the wood – five choices. Which one would he take?

Fiona switches off the engine and opens the car door. The cold of the night is cleaner than the cold of the day, but perhaps she is feeling it more sharply because she is wearing nightclothes. She waits by the gate and listens hard, but she can hear no footsteps.

She knows now that by locking it in she has forced the creature to pine for its freedom. If she hadn't been so afraid of losing it she could have helped it on this journey, offering it a key to the door which could, in time, have led to its return. But it was too late now. The creature had gone back into the wild. Fiona transmits her love across the darkness and prays to a God she had once known to keep it safe.

From behind a tree Billy watches the weeping woman get back into the car and drive away. He tries but can feel no sympathy for her. He is wearing his school uniform and his satchel. Billy has planned his escape in detail. He will move on in the morning under the cover of thousands of children going to school. He has fifty-seven pounds and forty pence in his pocket; the exact cost of the trainers that Fiona had bought for him and two weeks' pocket money. He had taken the money from her purse and left the receipt inside one of the trainers. That way she could return them to the shop and get her money back. He had taken nothing that didn't belong to him.

20

Jane wakes from a deep sleep in an unfamiliar bedroom. From the quality of the light it seems to be afternoon. She finds a linen shirt draped across her chest. His shirt. Of course. Now she remembers: she came back to his flat to confront Lucy. Lucy wasn't there, but Anthony was – and when she arrived he immediately went to buy some wine, telling her to make herself at home. He remembered her. She was surprised. More than ten years had passed since she had last seen him. When Anthony went out to buy the wine she went to sleep on his bed.

The front door of the flat slams. She sits up. She is fully dressed. Silently she gets out of bed and tiptoes to the door. Through the crack she sees Anthony come in. She rushes back to the bed and feigns sleep. She hears the bedroom door being gently opened and then pulled shut again. When

Anthony's footsteps have retreated, she gets up silently, goes to the door and pushes it until she can see into the living room. She sees Anthony slump onto the settee. He rubs his eyes with his palms; a gesture of tiredness and frustration. He stands again, goes to a cabinet and pours himself a large Scotch. Then he looks towards the bedroom door. Jane backs away but thinks he may have seen her. She discerns a minute change in his expression: a wince of memory. She sees the shirt on the bed, crumpled. She returns to it and straightens it, then goes back to the door and looks through the gap. Anthony is now at the table in the centre of the room. He has picked up the phone and he is dialling, still standing. The whisky glass is on the table.

'. . . It's me,' he says. It is a duty call. His voice is weary. '. . . Yes, yes, fine. You? . . . Is he? Well don't let him . . . No, I haven't seen Blacker . . . Apparently they're still holding him . . . No, well I'm afraid that we're not part of the due process . . .' During this exchange he takes the phone and the Scotch with him and sits down on the settee again, with his back to Jane.

Jane opens the door and walks into the lounge. Silently she approaches and stands behind him. Anthony's neck is quite visible to her, his head bent with weariness.

The phone call continues: '. . . No, I haven't been drinking. . . No, just tired . . . Look, when are you coming back? . . . Well ring National Rail now and get a cab when you get to this end . . . No, it's in the book I imagine . . . Well he must have a book somewhere. . . What? . . . Well of course it's no trouble . . . Sure. I'll call you back with it . . . Yes, I do understand . . . Well, it's hard for . . . No, I'm not . . .'

Jane reaches out and runs her nails against the exposed flesh of his neck. He reacts, recoils, shrugs off the shock of the contact. Jane walks around to face him. Anthony remains calm. Looking up towards her, he says: 'Lucy. Look, got to go. Somebody at the door. I'll call you with the number . . . Yes. OK . . . OK.' He puts down the phone.

'He didn't love her,' Jane says.

Anthony remains silent and seated. He takes a sip of his whisky. Jane walks slowly around the room. 'She didn't love him . . . and I know what you think.'

'Do you? What do I think?'

'I know you think I was just the other woman – the bit on the side – but it wasn't like that. It wasn't like that at all.'

'You know I'm trying to . . . trying to work out whether you coming back here is either grotesquely inappropriate or . . . or somehow absolutely in keeping with what I would have expected from my little brother. I was standing in the off-licence contemplating it and I just couldn't decide.'

'I don't know what you're talking about.'

'And that makes it even more absurd. Because you see all this . . . his death, solely in terms of its impact on you, don't you?'

'He loved me.'

'He fucked you. Over ten years ago. Several times. And then he ran away. Which, I might add, he had a habit of doing.'

'He didn't,' Jane says quietly. 'It wasn't like that.' She knew what anger and pain did to you; the ugly lies it made you tell. At least living with Hackett's temper had taught her that.

'So why don't you try and explain to me what it was like.'

'She used to hurt him. Did he tell you that? Once she broke one of his fingers . . . He said he loved me for my gentleness. I never hurt him.'

'No. He couldn't have been hurt by someone like you.'

'We had this place we'd . . . it didn't matter where we . . . the outside world didn't matter but it was like only the two of us had the key to it . . .'

'God preserve us.'

'. . . and that's where we'd meet. And people thought they could see us but they . . . They could see our bodies, but not what was going on in our heads. It was love and unless you've felt it like that, you just wouldn't understand.'

'Cloud Cuckoo Land I believe it's called.'

'You can't spoil it . . . I couldn't bear to see him keep going back to her. I just couldn't stand what it did to him.'

When the phone rings Jane picks it up. She listens to the voice for a moment then she hands it to Anthony.

'. . . Yes,' he says. '. . . Look I can't talk . . . Yes . . . it's quite difficult actually to talk at the moment . . . company, yes . . . well, her name is Jane and she's . . . Jane. That's right.' There is a long pause in which Jane sees a number of emotions expressed by Anthony's eyes: deepening shades of comprehension. Finally, as he turns his face to her, she hears him say: 'Perhaps that's true,' and then he hands the phone to

Jane, explaining: 'Lucy wants to talk to you.'

Jane takes the phone but does not put it immediately to her ear. It wasn't supposed to have happened like this. She had prepared herself for a confrontation with her but when Anthony had answered the door everything had gone from her mind. They had talked and then he had left her alone in the flat because he said he needed to go and get some wine. She thought that he was testing her, to see what she would do to the flat, but she didn't care. She had gone immediately to the bedroom, opened the wardrobe and buried her face in his clothes.

Anthony pours himself another Scotch. Jane holds the phone six inches away from her ear – listening.

'. . . No. No, it wasn't like that,' she says towards Anthony. '. . . No, you can't spoil it all now.' She slams the phone down. It rings again.

'Leave it,' Anthony says. It continues to ring until he goes to the wall and unplugs it. 'It seems that Lucy knew all about you.' He lays down the cable of the phone on the wooden floor. 'I thought I understood her. It seems that I don't . . . I think I admire her for . . . Should I? Is it admirable?'

'If somebody I loved was seeing somebody else and I found out about it, I'd kill them.'

'Yes, I expect you would.'

'I've got to go,' Jane says but makes no move towards the door.

'Must you?'

'I don't want to see her.'

'She won't be here for hours.'

'She's terrible.'

'Listen to me. For what it's worth I don't think I blame you.'

'Why should you blame me?'

'Perhaps I shouldn't. No, of course I shouldn't. Look. I don't . . . I don't know you at all, but I knew John quite well I believe and if you mattered to him then . . . and I don't know what goes on in that mind of yours but I gain some peace from the knowledge that he was loved by you . . . Now I know Luce has a temper. But I don't think it's particularly helpful given the current circumstances, to continue with these ridiculous allegations.'

Jane nods.

'So whatever you've told yourself, please be good enough to keep it to yourself. I neither want to know nor hear any more of it. Lucy is my sister-in-law and I love her and nothing you can tell me will change that. OK?'

Jane goes to the piano, sits on the stool and lifts the lid. Anthony approaches her and stands behind her – so close that she can feel his heat. She waits for him to reach out and touch her. When he does she doesn't recoil. His hand moves from her shoulder to her breast. She needs to feel the contact to see if there is anything of him in it, but there isn't and she is glad. She pushes away the dead weight of his hand. She is grateful that he doesn't resist.

'Sometimes,' she says. 'When I was holding Billy it was like I was holding him.'

'Billy?'

'My boy.'

'Your son?'

'My little soldier.'

'He's not . . . you're not suggesting he's . . .?'

Jane takes one further look around the flat and lets herself out. For some time Anthony remains standing beside the piano. Since his brother's death he hasn't been able to bring himself to play it. He feels the warmth of the whisky at the top of his chest. When he takes a further sip the heat spreads down to cloak his lungs. He swallows and the warmth seeps slowly away. Having felt little but shock since his brother's death he is surprised that he is capable of feeling what he recognizes as gratitude. Throughout the narrative of this tragedy – his brother's disappearance; the discovery of the body; the arrest of the man; the carefully worded questions from Blacker, the CID man, about the nature of his brother's sexuality; the revelation of the witness; the discovery in the suspect's flat of his brother's belongings – through all that, part of him remained as objective as it had always been. It is that part of him which will enjoy Lucy's reaction when he tells her that her husband has fathered a bastard child.

21

Only when Billy approaches the front door does his certainty falter. The journey had been straightforward. A train ride and then a bus. He had achieved his objective having asked for help only once, and that had been when he had nearly reached his destination. He got off the bus at a stop one road away from the address he had been looking for; the conductor had grudgingly given him directions.

Billy looks down at two, filthy milk bottles on the front step. Both have mustard coloured mould in them. He can smell that it is the house of a smoker – or several smokers. The door is half glass. The crimson glass panel on the right has been broken and cardboard has been taped over it. The central panel is royal blue. A piece of paper has been stuck over the circular bell-press with a pencil note saying 'Bell not working. Please knock'. Billy looks up when he hears a sudden flush of water. A bath has been emptied and suds splash onto the path from a leaking joint in the metal down-pipe. The water smells sweetly of lavender. Billy steps back and continues to peer up at the red-bricked face of the building. It is three storeys high and he tries to imagine on which floor his mother would live. If she had a choice she would be on the ground floor. But somehow he knows she is not on the ground floor because the net curtains obscuring the rooms on each side of the front door are yellow with age and filth and he knows that she would not allow them to get that way. The address on his chocolate wrapper is 'Flat 4'. There's no bell to ring at Flat 4, so he decides his only option is to knock on the heavy door – which he does, without much hope of attracting the attention of anybody inside.

He knocks again, then, making blinkers of his hands, peers through the coloured glass. The hallway is dark and there is no movement inside. With his nose pressed to the door he can smell traffic and smoke. He decides to peel away the damp cardboard. If he sees somebody moving around inside he will call out to let them know he is here. Under normal circumstances he wouldn't do such a thing for the fear of punishment would be too great. But the conventions he has lived by with Fiona and Don no longer apply; there is no figure of authority whose punishment would count. Billy has never been afraid of pain, but Fiona held a more effective weapon – the threat of removing his limited access to his mother. She used it often.

The cardboard comes away easily enough and the jagged-edged hole in the glass is large enough for him to get his left hand through. His slender fingers soon locate the Yale lock a few inches to the right of it. The door swings open and he faces the hallway.

Taking a step inside Billy waits for a moment before shutting the door behind him. A loud, powerful car passes on the street obliterating his thoughts. When the noise of it has gone he strains to listen for signs of habitation. He can hear a radio playing from a room above but nothing from the ground floor. He walks towards the broad staircase and passes a door on the right which is labelled 'Flat 1: Burgess'. Across the corridor is Flat 2, but the corridor continues past the stairs towards another door which is unlabelled. He returns to the staircase and looks up. The house above him seems vast: the ceilings are high; there are areas of straight-edged shadow and pools of milky light on the walls. A piercing white ray of afternoon sun bisects the landing. A dusty chandelier is suspended from the ceiling at the top of the house. It looks like a creature Billy once saw in a programme about the deep. He wills himself to climb the stairs but for the first time he feels afraid: the further away he is from the front door, the greater the danger. It's an old fear of being trapped and held against his will, but actually worrying about it distracts him sufficiently and soon he is at the top of the stairs.

He looks back into the hallway, a steep fall below him – like standing on the highest board at the swimming pool.

Fiona and Don had taken him swimming soon after he had arrived at their house. In the first few weeks he spent there, when they went out it was only as a 'family'. Fiona, he learned from overhearing a whispered conversation, was worried he would run away if Don wasn't accompanying them. So they had gone to the local pool and Don had taken him into the changing room and they had both put on their trunks in a small cubicle. Don seemed unashamed of his nakedness, but Billy had turned his back to him to undress. Wearing the trunks his mother had bought him made him sad. She would occasionally send a parcel of clothes via the social worker and sometimes he would be allowed to open it. He climbed the steps to the top board to show Don how brave he was but he doubted anybody could have jumped or dived from that height and survived. He climbed down again, catching sight of Fiona who was sitting halfway up the tiered seats at the side with a magazine on her knee. She looked hot and bored. They had stopped on the way home to get an ice cream. It was supposed to be a treat but ice cream wasn't a treat. Billy often had it for pudding when he lived with his mother. She told him you could buy it cheap from Iceland. He was glad he didn't have to pretend to be grateful any longer.

The lino on the corridor floor is scarred with cigarette burns. The radio is louder here and he can now hear a budgerigar singing. Flat 3 is watching afternoon television; a cook explains what he is going to do to some turnips. A man chips in. An audience laughs at the innuendo. Billy reaches Flat 4 and his stomach feels tight. He can hear a television inside: it sounds like horse-racing commentary. He knocks and while he waits he straightens his satchel and brushes his hair straight. His face feels greasy because he hasn't been able to wash it today. He hears a cough from inside and it doesn't sound like his mother, it sounds like a very old lady. The door opens and he is overwhelmed by the smell of cigarette smoke. The woman who has come to the door is wearing a nylon housecoat. She has a cigarette in her right hand, which he can see is shaking a little.

'Yes?' she says. She seems suspicious of him, but Billy senses she is glad at his intrusion. He doesn't know what to do or say. He had not anticipated his mother would not be at the address she had given him.

'What do you want, dear?' the woman says more gently. She looks anxiously over her shoulder towards a man who is sitting in deep shadow in the room behind her watching the television.

'Who is it?' the man calls.

'It's a boy.'

'Tell him we don't give to the scouts.'

'You're not the scouts, are you?' she asks. Billy shakes his head.

'. . . and he can piss off if he thinks we're having raffle tickets off him.'

The woman smiles: Billy feels she is on his side and not on the side of the man in the room.

'Are you collecting?' the woman asks him quietly, then

draws deeply on her cigarette. 'Cancer?'

'No.'

'So do I have to guess then why you're standing at my door or are you going to tell me?'

'I've got the wrong address,' Billy says.

'What flat are you looking for?'

'Flat 4.'

'Well, this is Flat 4 . . .'

'Oh,' Billy says.

'I could give you a drink of orange if you like.'

'Is he still there?' the man calls.

'Would you like a drink of orange?'

Billy nods. He has no other options to pursue. The woman stands aside and Billy walks into the living room. The man jacks his face towards him. His neck seems stiff. His eyes blaze with anger at the intrusion. The curtains are drawn to improve the picture on the television but Billy can see the man is smartly dressed in a white shirt and dark trousers which have a stiff crease in them.

'Fuck me. You let him in,' the man says. He shakes his head and grabs the arms of the chair as if he is afraid of falling out sideways. Billy now sees two oxygen cylinders on a trolley against the wall. On the floor beside the man's chair is a large bottle of beer. Billy thinks it is the saddest room he has ever seen.

'You're an easy touch,' the man says.

'He's lost,' the woman explains. Billy stands between them.

'How can he be lost? How can anybody be lost I'd like to know. Eh?'

'He's been given an address but it's the wrong one. Isn't it?'

'Yes,' Billy says.

'Who by?'

'I don't know. It doesn't matter who gave it him, all that matters is that it's the wrong one.'

'So he's not lost then. He knows where he is but it's not where he wants to be.'

'Your mind,' the woman says with wonder. 'The way it works.'

'At least it fucking works. Which is more than I can say about some people.'

'I think he's referring to me,' the woman tells Billy. 'But you won't have to mind him. I don't. He's in constant pain.'

'You're telling me I'm in constant pain. Bloody earache from listening to you, going on all day.' The man tears his attention from the television screen again and looks towards Billy. 'I can't see you over there. Come and sit over here where I can see you.'

Billy feels no menace from the couple. His instincts for danger, sharpened in many dangerous circumstances, suggest to him that there is comfort to be found in this smelly, sad room with the thin old lady and the grumpy old man.

'I'll get your orange and we'll see if we can find a biscuit,' the woman says as she goes away through a nicotine-stained door.

'Get him some pop,' the man shouts. 'Pop all right? Boys like pop.'

'Don't mind,' Billy says.

'We haven't got any pop,' the woman calls back. 'He'll have to have orange or lime juice cordial . . . or tonic.'

'He won't have tonic. It's too bitter.'

'He'll have orange then. That's what he wanted.'

They wait in silence until she re-emerges. The man has lost interest in Billy now that another race has started on the television. He shows no emotion but at the race's conclusion he turns back towards Billy and sees that he is now holding a glass of orange juice. The woman stands behind him.

'You interested in the gee-gees?' he asks.

'Not really.'

'Best keep it that way. Cost you a fortune, it will.'

'He doesn't bet,' the woman explains. 'Not with money.'

'She doesn't know what I do,' he whispers. 'Sneak out of here when she's not looking. Down the bookies. Fifty quid on the nose. Bish-bosh. Back before she even knows I'm gone.'

'That's right. Down the bookies on his magic broomstick with his oxygen and somebody to wipe his nose when he . . .'

'All right, don't go on.'

'It's not me who's . . .'

'The boy's getting bored with you going on – aren't you?'

'No,' Billy says truthfully.

'Do I know you?' The old man eyes Billy with more interest.

'No.'

'You been round here before on the scrounge?'

'No. I don't live here.'

'Deliver the free-sheet, then? Is that it?'

'No.'

'Only you look familiar. Does he look familiar?' he asks the woman.

'Not to me.'

'. . . Fuck me,' he says. 'Fuck me.'

'He's not usually this bad,' the woman explains to Billy.

'No. Not that. Not that. I've just seen it.'

'Seen what?'

'Look at him. Look at the boy.'

'I don't know what you're talking about.' To Billy, she says 'he's like this sometimes. He thinks he's two steps ahead of me, but usually he's two steps behind.'

'Just look at him.' The man says again. The woman shakes her head.

'Well if you can't see it, I'm not going to tell you.' He is looking at the shrine on the mantelpiece: a photo of a boy standing beside his mother and behind them is a jungle scene. In front of the photograph is a candle that has never been lit.

'You're crackers, Hackett,' the woman says. 'Do you know that? A fruit-and-nutcase.'

22

'When you stir the water, it makes a well in the middle. Drop the egg – which you've already broken into a cup – into this well and the egg will form into a teardrop shape.' Jane hears the instructions in her head as she breaks the egg straight into the boiling water. White tentacles immediately shoot to the edge of the pan, the water bubbles over the side and the orange electric ring hisses. A smell of burning fills the kitchen. She slides the small pan onto a cold ring and watches the water settle to a lower level. The yolky eye of the poaching egg lies just beneath the surface in a pool of murky water.

When you stir the water, how long does it keep circling for, she wonders. For ages, probably. For hours and hours and hours. She looks closely at it to test her assumption but it seems to be still. Perhaps it continues to move at the bottom but is invisible to the naked eye. Jane realizes she has forgotten to put the toast under the grill. Opening the bag, she finds the bread is stale, but she doesn't mind stale bread for toast. When she puts the bread beneath the grill she sees the scratch on her arm. It is red and new; a long, thin, valley of flesh.

It was dark by the time *she* got out of the taxi, paid the driver through the window, and came into the hallway where Jane was waiting, shivering in the cold. She had been there for four hours. Neither said anything immediately. Lucy was carrying a leather holdall which seemed very full. She turned to the letterbox vault. Jane didn't move but just stood there watching her.

After a moment, Lucy said, 'It's you, isn't it?' and Jane nodded. 'Why did you come?' Lucy put down her holdall and ran her hand through her hair. She was growing it out and it looked a mess, which disadvantaged her.

'I wanted to see you.'

They came from different worlds but, instinctively, at that moment, Jane felt she knew every thought that was going through Lucy's head. As such, the conversation was already over, her curiosity was satisfied and she could go back to her flat and get on with her life.

'For what reason?' Lucy asked her.

Blah, blah, blah, Jane thought. Blah, blah. But she didn't say it because she didn't want to appear rude. So what she said was: 'I just wanted to see you.'

'. . . You're not what I expected.'

The women looked at each other for a moment, wondering what the man they had shared had found appealing in the other. Jane was tall and thin with a delicate beauty. Lucy was short and what Jane would have called fat – though Lucy would have argued that she was only temporarily overweight. Jane was unhappy and angry and sometimes not quite sane. Lucy was unhappy and angry but her sanity had never been questioned. Jane had once told the Sugar Plum Fairy that she often felt she was on a boat far out to sea, but she could see – in the distance – the cliffs. The boat was heading home and at the top of the cliffs lay her happiness. Rocks stood ahead of them though and the cliff face was steep. A lighthouse warned her away. Jane would have said that Lucy's cliffs were behind her and she was sailing away from shore. Poor Lucy, Jane thought, knowing how much she would have hated to be pitied by her.

Jane turned and went out of the hallway. After being inside for so long she was glad to feel the open space of the city around her: the noise of traffic, the planes blinking in the sky. She didn't even mind the cold. When she looked back she could see that Lucy had followed her out. She seemed small and vulnerable against the large night sky. Jane wondered whether she should wait for her to catch up, but decided they had nothing more to say. Only then did it occur to her that the other woman might have good cause to be angry with her. Whatever the rights and wrongs of it all Lucy was, after all, his wife.

They continued to walk through the front gardens

towards the street. Jane accelerated but she could hear Lucy's hard heels tapping quickly on the street. She knew she could run and escape – Lucy would be too dignified to run after her – or she could wait and allow her to say what she wanted to say. Curiosity compelled her to wait. She had nothing more to lose. If Lucy tried to hit her, she felt she would be able to stand up for herself. While she waited for her to catch up, she saw Lucy get out her mobile phone and dial. As she did so, she looked back towards the flats. It seemed there was no reply because she returned her phone to her handbag.

There are two sharp knocks at Jane's door. She is angry with herself for not bandaging the cut on her arm. Any normal person would have tended to it immediately. But the cut was interesting to her both in the way it looked and how the pain of it changed when she twisted her arm. It hurt as much as when Lucy had first done it to her. But it was too late to sort it out now. Perhaps it would be Alf at the door or Maude and she could ask them to come back in a moment. Or perhaps Ian the plumber had come to see her because he couldn't keep away. Jane opens the door to a policeman and policewoman.

'Exactly how do you know Anthony?' Lucy asked her when she reached her.

'He's John's brother,' Jane explained. It seemed simple enough, but of course it wasn't, because of the implications.

'So you knew Anthony before John was killed?'

'I didn't know him,' Jane said. 'Not like I know Patrick.'

'Patrick?'

'Yes. At the bookshop.'

'But he knew about you?'

'Yes. Well, I met him once.'

'I see,' Lucy said, and nodded her head as she took this in. 'You weren't the only one. With John. There were others.'

This silenced Jane.

'Did you think you were? Of course you did. Why wouldn't you?'

What Jane wanted to say to Lucy was how much John had hated her; he hadn't loved her, he had been afraid of her. But she thought it would seem petty and she no longer wanted to hurt Lucy, she just wanted to go away and never see her again. If John had known other women then so what? – he would never have loved anybody the way he loved her. She knew about the arrogance of love. That was what made it such a powerful emotion. The arrogance made you certain and lifted you up above everybody else in the world. Being in love like that allowed no space for anyone else to get in.

'You didn't know him,' Jane allowed herself to say. But it was the worst thing she could have said because Lucy made a quick snort and her hand went to her mouth, as though she had drunk something and it had gone down the wrong way.

'. . . I'm sure you'd love to see yourself as the naïve injured

193

party in all this, but things are never black and white are they?'

'That's what you want to believe.'

'So he framed me as the jealous, obsessive wife, yes?'

'He loved me. You don't know the truth.'

'I don't think you're interested in the truth. Even if you could recognize it. Which I very much doubt.'

'You broke his finger.'

'He told you that, did he? And how exactly did he say I did it?'

'Your temper.'

'Accident. In a car door. He slammed it in a hissy fit. But that doesn't make him out to be the victim, does it, Jane? And he did like to make himself out to be the victim.'

'Jane Hackett?' the policewoman says. Jane instinctively covers the cut on her arm with her palm. The sudden movement makes the policewoman take a step away from her. The policeman beside her, no more than a youth, looks confused: he isn't sure if action is required so he tenses and monitors his colleague's reactions, prepared to follow her lead if it is.

'Can we come in?' she asks. Jane notices that the policewoman has already scanned the room behind her. She feels sick with apprehension. Surely they haven't come to take her away again? Perhaps they have made new laws and she has fallen foul of them by mistake. She decides to go along with them; bide her time, be polite and do what normal people would: offer them a cup of tea and show them that she is just a normal person who has rights and who lives in a flat and who does her laundry and who doesn't make the place too messy.

'Yes. Come in,' Jane says and lets them walk past her. She has nothing to hide. She follows them in and tries to see the small flat as they would be seeing it. It's not her fault if this is all she can afford, just as it wasn't her fault that the water boiled over when she put the egg in it. And if they hadn't come to the door then, the room wouldn't be full of smoke from the toast that has just burnt under the grill.

'Do you want to – ah – do something about that, Miss?' the young policeman says, but the policewoman is sure enough of herself to go to the grill, pull out the tray and tip the two slices of blackened toast into the bin.

'You might want to open the window,' she suggests to the policeman. He can have witnessed no hell, yet, Jane thinks. She has never seen such innocence in the face of a man.

'Right.' He is glad to be of some practical use. Approaching the sash, he opens his arms wide as if he is roughly measuring the width for new glass. The window is stiff but in a moment he has slid it up. While Jane goes to sit on her settee, her hands in her lap, he peers out of the window looking up towards the bottom of the rotten frame. But she has fallen into old habits. The two intruders have taken over her flat and she is powerless again. She wishes she knew what she could do to stop things like this happening: surely a woman like Lucy wouldn't allow a policewoman to come in without any reason and throw away her toast without permission.

'What did you do to your arm?' the policewoman asks her. She looks pointedly towards her colleague to make sure he has not missed the significance of it.

'I scratched it,' Jane says. 'It's not a crime, is it?'

The policeman laughs. The policewoman looks at him coldly. You won't last long, Jane thinks. She now knows she should have asked them what they wanted when they arrived. By letting them in without question she has pleaded guilty to whatever crime they have come to accuse her of.

'What do you want?' Jane asks. 'Here. Coming here to harass me in my own flat.'

'We're not here to harass you. We're making enquiries about a boy,' the policewoman says.

'What boy?' Jane knows no boys who commit crimes. Only men.

'We thought you might be able to tell us.'

'Look. I . . . I don't know what I'm supposed to have done. So can you tell me please. And then leave.'

'I think he's known to you as Billy.'

'Billy!' Jane crosses the room before the woman has had the chance to register that she has moved. 'What do you mean Billy? What's happened to Billy?'

'Hold her,' the policewoman orders the man, and then there is a tussle as he tries to pin Jane's arms to her side. But because he tries to achieve it without hurting her, he forgets the lessons he learned in the gym and Jane keeps struggling free. She is fighting to get at the policewoman. Something in her head is telling her that to get the information she needs out of the woman, she needs to slap it out of her. To knock her down and kick her until she stops moving. To tear out her eyes. The woman folds her arms and watches Jane's rage burn out as the policeman controls her. He discovers eventually that all he needs to do is to embrace her, and so they stand, Jane in his arms, until her sobbing subsides. He smiles in apology towards his colleague but he is enjoying the rare moment of intimacy.

Time passes because the next thing Jane knows is that again she is sitting on the settee. She has a glass of water in her hand. The policeman is sitting next to her, with his helmet on his lap, and the woman is standing and calmly explaining to her that Billy has disappeared from his foster parents.

'When?' Jane asks in a shaking voice.

'Early hours of this morning. His mother saw him walking off down the street and gave chase in the car but he eluded her.'

'She's not his mother,' Jane says dully. 'I'm his mother. If he was still with me he wouldn't need to be running away.'

'Well, that's as may be. We're not here to sit in judgement over the rights and wrongs of the case; we're tasked with finding the boy and returning him to his rightful home.'

Jane feels so broken that she doesn't have the energy to take on the policewoman again.

'. . . I'm going to leave you a number,' the woman says.

'And if you hear anything I want you to call me and tell me. If I'm not there, whoever answers will be able to get a message to me . . . understand?' She hands Jane a card. 'Come on, Rowse,' she says to the man who stands, reluctantly.

'He'll be all right,' Rowse assures her. 'When I was a boy I was always running away.'

'You don't seem the type,' Jane says.

'My dad was always in his shed.'

'That's enough!' The policewoman nods the policeman through the door ahead of her. He has to dip to get his head under the frame because he has put his helmet on. 'And if he does turn up here don't keep it to yourself. You won't be doing him any favours.'

'No, I don't suppose I will.'

'. . . Don't worry,' Rowse says. 'We'll find him.'

When Jane takes a sip of the water in the glass it is warm because she has been holding it in her hand for three hours. Her body is tense, her hearing alert to the sound in the corridor of a boy's footsteps. But how would he know where to come? He doesn't know her address.

The cut on her arm is stinging. The valley of flesh has become deeper. How did she get it?

This is how: as Jane backed away from Lucy, she stumbled. Lucy reached out to stop her falling but her nail caught Jane's arm. As Jane ran, she could hear the other woman calling after her. She seemed concerned for her. But Jane had had it all planned. It wasn't supposed to have happened like that. She set out to hurt Lucy and she ended up being hurt herself. She set out hating her and ended up feeling sorry for her. She set out looking for something for herself but too late she realized she didn't know what it was, so she couldn't find it. Tough-titty, Jane.

Tough-titty.

23

Billy watches the old man as he moves a thick white candle aside and picks up the framed photograph which stands behind it on the mantelpiece. Holding it at arm's length he stares at it, then back towards the boy. From behind him, Billy hears the old woman say, 'My God.'

'I think we owe him a few quid in pocket-money, don't we?' The old man wipes a film of dust from the photograph with the cuff of his shirt.

'My God,' the woman says again.

'You'd better tell him.' The old man returns to his chair and sits heavily. 'It'll sound better coming from you.' He points the remote control at the television and the set pings off. Billy swivels around to look at the old woman who is behind him in the shadows. Her expression has quietened and hardened.

'You tell him. I can't do it.'

'Coward.'

When the woman leaves the room it is through a door Billy hasn't noticed before – like a secret exit from a library which is opened by pushing a row of fake books.

'She's upset,' the old man says without compassion. 'She'll be out soon enough. It's all come as a bit of a shock to her.' The photograph is on his knee, face down. '. . . I expect you're wondering what all this palaver is about.'

Afterwards, Billy thought he should have understood sooner. It was clear that the old couple knew more about him than he did about them, but that wasn't surprising because he didn't know anything beyond what he'd picked up from the clues in the room. He wondered, though, as he sat on the settee, with the grumpy old man close-by giving off a smell of stale beer, and the black china bowl of over-ripe bananas on the sideboard behind him, why it all seemed comfortable to him; why he knew it without knowing it. There had always been places he felt like this: at the corners of parks, certain places in school corridors, a waiting-room at a railway station where he remembered sitting with his mother when he was very young. It was a small country halt just next to a tunnel opening. It had been raining and he felt as though he could have stayed there for ever and been happy. The rain stopped before the train came and the sun came out but it wasn't the same; the rain was an important part of the feeling.

When the old man leans across the space between them

and hands him the photograph frame, Billy takes it in both hands and places it, face-up, across his knees. The photograph is one he knows: he and his mother taken at a photographic studio. They are standing in front of a big jungle frieze. Billy and his mother had spotted the edge of the jungle background behind the sombre blue curtain the photographer had tugged across the bare wall behind them. Both had insisted that he replace the curtain with the frieze. In the photograph his mother's hand is resting gently on his shoulder. She is wearing a belted cotton dress and very bright red lipstick which matches her high-heeled shoes. At the time her hair was long with a side parting. He is wearing his school shirt and shorts but not his glasses. When they told the photographer that they wanted him to make them look like jungle explorers, he went off to find his stuffed parrot.

Billy remembers the day for another reason: because his mother had made a fuss when she was presented with the bill. She had taken a voucher with them from the local paper which she said meant the photo should have been free. The sweaty, jovial man in the brightly coloured waistcoat, whose business it was and who had taken their picture, explained that if she had read the small print she would have seen that she had to buy a large photo at full price; only then would the second one be free. He wasn't running a charity, he said, and laughed at the absurdity of the suggestion, expecting Jane to join in. Her hysteria had won the battle because there had been a large family in the waiting room and the father

– alerted by the shouting – had popped his bald head through the beaded curtain to ask if everything was all right. 'You're twisted,' the photographer said to his mother as they left. Billy remembered the words because they made him think of a human maypole. The man hadn't seemed to intend it as an insult, just an observation. Billy felt sorry for him after that because it had taken him ages to find the parrot. He had gone up to his flat above the studio and when he had come down again he was very red-faced and said he'd tracked it down in the attic. When he'd brought it in he'd put it on Billy's shoulder and pretended it was saying 'pieces of eight'. Billy knew he was just trying to impress his mother because he thought she was pretty.

There had been many such moments in his life; public confrontations which left him feeling guilty and afraid. The fear would retreat after a while, but he was always left wondering who was right and who was wrong. He never forgot the faces of the people his mother had hurt or made angry, or sometimes cry; he took a share of the burden of guilt on himself even though he knew it probably didn't belong to him. He felt sorry for the parrot-man because he didn't seem to know how to stand up for himself – which was strange, because Billy had always assumed that when you were a grown-up everything would be much easier.

'Well?' the grumpy old man says. 'Recognize it?'

'Yes.' Billy holds the frame out for the man to take it from him.

'Put it back up there for me.' Hackett nods his head towards the mantelpiece. When Billy stands up and carefully places it back in position he is aware of the man watching him. There are two other photographs on the dusty shelf. One is in black and white and shows a woman in a swimsuit beside a swimming pool. Another is in old-fashioned colour and shows a younger version of the old couple in a blizzard of confetti on the steps of a building.

'It just went on too long,' Billy hears the old man say. He is addressing the thin old woman who is back in the room again. She is holding a folded handkerchief and she has lit another cigarette. Billy returns to the settee.

'That was your pride,' the woman says.

'Pride? No. It wasn't pride.'

'What then?'

'Guilt? You name it.'

'You don't know guilt, Hackett.'

'I know guilt.'

'. . . He doesn't know about us,' the old woman says to Hackett. 'I always wondered if she'd tell him we were alive.'

'Do you blame her?'

'No, I don't blame her. But I wonder what he's doing here now.'

'She gave him the address, that's what he's doing here now.'

'You say your mum gave you the address, did she?' the woman asks Billy.

'Yes.' It doesn't matter to Billy that he doesn't understand what's going on; all that matters is that it doesn't threaten him. Then he remembers the other detail: 'She wrote it on a chocolate wrapper.'

'She always liked her chocolate,' the old woman says with disapproval. 'But why here? That's what I don't understand. Why did she give him our address?'

'You know what she's like.'

'I did. Only you forget.'

'What did she say to you when she gave you the address?' Hackett asks Billy.

'Don't know.'

'Don't know? You don't know much, do you.'

'I don't remember.'

'So she didn't give it to you recently?' the old woman tries.

'No. Last year.'

'Last year? Well you weren't in a hurry to get here, were you?' Hackett says.

'I only found it last week.'

'And you thought it was her address?'

'Yes.'

'So you don't live with your mother?' This question comes from the old lady. Billy's neck is becoming stiff from turning to look from one to the other.

'No.' He decides not to offer any more information until he knows more about them.

'. . . Fetch me another bottle of beer, will you?' Hackett says.

'I don't think there is another.'

'That's no good. We should be celebrating.'

'You're always celebrating.'

'Drowning my sorrows more like.'

'. . . Why did you leave it so long before you came to see us?' the old woman asks.

'I only found it last week.'

'And you thought it was your mum's address?'

'He already said that, didn't he?' Hackett says. 'Strewth. You call me a fruit-and-nutcase . . . Well? Are you going to tell him or shall I?'

While Billy waits, the old lady comes from behind him. When he looks up towards her he can see her eyes have filled with tears. She wipes them away with the handkerchief she has balled in her right hand, then she sits beside him and takes his right hand.

'Billy,' she says. 'I'm your Nan. And this is your Granddad.' Billy and the old woman look towards Hackett who holds up an empty glass.

'Cheers,' he says. 'Welcome to the family.'

'I expect you want to think about this for a bit, don't you?'

'Does that mean I can stay here?' Billy says.

'Would you like to stay here?'

'Yes. Until we go and see my mum.'

'I don't know about that,' Hackett says. 'Where have you come from?'

'He can stay here for a bit. Surely he can,' the woman says.

'I mean we're his grandparents. Nobody's going to get funny about a lad spending a night with his Nan and Granddad.'

'You don't know that. You read about people being had up all the time for messing with children.'

'Not grandparents.'

'Even them . . . He'll have to sleep in here.'

'I can make up a bed for him.'

'What if I have to get up in the night?'

'Yes, Billy,' the woman says. 'You can stay the night here. We'd be very glad to have you – wouldn't we Hackett?'

'We could take him to the pub. Would Trevor let him in, do you reckon?'

'He's not going to any pub. He's staying in and we're going to have a nice sit-down meal together and he's going to tell us all about himself. Isn't that right, Billy?'

'Yes.'

'Get some fish and chips. Take him with you. He'd like that,' Hackett says.

'Do you like fish and chips?'

'I don't like vinegar.'

'Get two large Haddock and two small bags of chips. That'll be enough for the three of us. They always give you too much at that Chink place. And some mushy peas . . . he's not saying much, is he? Considering.'

'He's thinking.' The old woman holds Billy's hand harder.

But Billy isn't thinking. He is content because, for the first time he can remember, he feels safe and the ball of anxiety in his stomach has shrunk. He doesn't know whether he should feel happier than he does at meeting the two old people. He doesn't even know if he is in some way guilty for not having known about them sooner. But, for the time being at least, he seems to be in the company of two people who are on his side.

24

After being visited by the police and then worrying for an hour, Jane decides to go and see the Sugar Plum Fairy. Apart from Patrick, whose shop is now closed because they are renovating it, she was the only person Jane could think of who would understand her fears over Billy's disappearance. Her only concern was that on the two previous occasions they had met they had parted after an argument. This had never happened while they were in the hospital together; on the ward they saved their wrath for the staff.

Jane remembers, as she gets off the single-decker bendy bus, that in the outside world the Sugar Plum Fairy is called Sharmini, although once she told Jane to call her Peaches. Jane checks this out by greeting her as Sharmini when she opens the door and turns on the porch light to see who is visiting her in the early evening gloom. It is immediately apparent that the Sugar Plum Fairy doesn't seem very pleased to see her. Sometimes, when Jane encounters people that she has known in the hospital, she doesn't acknowledge them because of the associations. But Sharmini stops short of making an excuse to get rid of Jane and grudgingly invites her in, saying: 'I'm making some lasagne for supper. You'd better come into the kitchen.'

Jane follows her through the cluttered communal living room. She skirts a bicycle which leans against the back of the settee on which a spruce, lean, elderly man is sitting with a large biscuit tin on his knee. He is wearing a trilby and a shiny, silver-grey suit and staring at the television, which is turned off.

'He's a Pole,' Sharmini confides when they reach the kitchen. 'We call him Colonel Ovkis because we can't say his name. He gets cross but Charlotte says he should speak more slowly.' Jane looks back through the kitchen door and sees that the Colonel is sitting stock-still under the pale cone of light from a standard lamp. '. . . Anyway, he's only been out for a few weeks. He doesn't have much English, but I don't think he wants to talk to anybody anyway.'

'Have you tried?'

'Yes. We have tried to draw him out of himself but the only thing he really gets excited about is talking about women kissing each other. "Go on," he says, "Lady kiss lady." He's an old perv, I think. But Charlotte might be a lezzer so she doesn't mind him so much.'

'Perhaps he's just lonely.'

'Some people deserve to be.'

'Nobody deserves to be lonely.'

'He's got a car though, and he seems happy to take us all out for a drive. We all went out for a McDonald's the other day – it was a drive-through one – but when we got to the booth nobody could make up their mind what they wanted so we all ended up shouting at each other, and a vicar kept pipping us so we went home. We don't know what he's got in that tin. Not biscuits.'

From their hospital conversations, Jane knows that Sharmini's messy, charmless dwelling is a half-way hostel run by a charity. She once told her that she had been there for so long she had forgotten where the other half was supposed to be. She made it out to be a joke but Jane could see that underneath it all she meant it. On the last occasion she had dropped in, there had been a disturbed girl who wouldn't come out of the bathroom (perhaps that was the Charlotte she had mentioned) and a woman in a fur coat who noisily dominated all the conversations. It was the woman in the coat who had provoked the row between them – but Jane couldn't remember what it had been about.

'It's my turn to cook tonight, so I decided to make some nettle lasagne,' Sharmini says, peering into a large saucepan from which protrude several nettle stalks. 'It doesn't seem to be doing anything. Have you ever cooked it?'

'Nettles? No. It sounds a bit strange.'

'I thought it might save me some money only I got all stung when I went out picking it – and I had to wash it thoroughly to get all the dog-piss off it. Dogs can't get stung on their winkies I suppose.'

'Don't you have a recipe?'

'No. I saw it in the paper once, and I decided to do it how I remembered it. But in the paper it was all smooth and thick and this isn't. I'll have to use the potato masher on them and then fry them up with some tinned tomatoes.'

'It might take more time.'

'I'll leave it with the lid on and have a ciggy. I can't offer you a drink because we don't have anything in . . . Well Colonel Ovkis has got some vodka in his room but he doesn't share it out.'

'That's all right.'

'You could have a cup of coffee. We got some free samples through the door yesterday. And Charlotte found a box of them in a skip. I don't think we've got any real milk.'

'No, I'm fine.'

'Well, sit down then.'

Jane sits at the kitchen table and Sharmini takes the chair facing her. Neither woman is comfortable in the company of the other, but Jane hopes that she doesn't look as bad as her friend who seems to have put on weight and has dyed her lank hair pink. Her knee-length dress is crimson; under it she is wearing green ballet tights.

'So have you been back in?' Sharmini asks, striking a match, squinting her right eye, and puckering her cracked lips to suck the flame into a long cigarette.

'Yes. I came out . . . a few days ago I think.'

'You seem all right at the moment. Are you all right?'

'I feel a bit slow – but I think I'm all right. Are you?'

'Yes. I'm trying some new tablets and they seem to be working but I'm putting on weight. You can't win, can you?'

'I don't know how it all happened. Usually I can remember but this time it's all blurry.'

'You didn't go in of your own accord?'

'No. I don't think so.'

'Last time they took me in I was reciting poetry outside the bank. No, that was the time before. This time I was reading a story I'd written and they called the police.'

'That seems a bit cruel.'

'The policeman said he'd arrested people for less. He was trying to be funny so I went for him with my nail scissors. I think that's why they took me in. Not for the story. I'll find it and let you have a read of it.'

'What was it about?'

'It was about a woman-teacher at a school who goes on a school trip up to London with a group of kids.'

'Go on.'

'. . . Well they're going to the theatre because they're studying Shakespeare. Anyway, she lives on her own but she really fancies this man-teacher who's on the trip with them. They're both quite old. Early fifties. So they get talking and everything goes all right although he doesn't seem very interested in her. But when they sit in the theatre he holds her hand all through the play. Afterwards, when the lights come up, he doesn't say anything and they go back home on the train again. His wife meets him at the station in their car and drives him off and she has to go home on her own. He doesn't offer her a lift. Pig.'

'How do the children get home from the station?'

'I don't go into that. They get picked up by their parents I suppose. Or carers.'

'And what happens then?'

'Nothing. You have to draw your own conclusions.'

'I think I need things spelling out for me.'

'People generally do.'

'I don't think I used to.'

Sharmini looks at her with disdain and takes another pull on her cigarette. 'So what brings you here?'

'You see – that's just what happens to me. I came here for an important reason and until you asked me I'd completely forgotten what it was. I couldn't think of anywhere else to go. I hope you don't mind.'

'I don't mind.'

'Billy's gone.'

'Piss and shit!'

'I know!'

'Gone where? I thought he was an adopted.'

'No – fostered. At the moment anyway.'

'Well either way I thought they were supposed to look after them.'

'That's what I thought. But he ran away.'

Sharmini shakes her head. From past experience, Jane knows that at this point she will either say something very helpful and sympathetic or begin a long rant directed towards whoever it is she has nominated to bear the blame. In the Sugar Plum Fairy's world there are only the blamed and the blameless: the blameless being the easy prey of the blamed, the blamed being all figures of authority, the government, men (mostly), women who use money ostentatiously i.e. who drive cars and dress well, and 'orientals'.

'So when did he go?' Sharmini asks, taking a deep drag.

'I don't know. Recently. Because the police came round today and I think they would have come quickly.'

'Mmm. Immediately, knowing them.' As Sharmini ruminates she chews her lower lip. She then stands and goes to the stove where she lifts the lid on the saucepan and looks inside.

'Actually it was the early hours of the morning. That's right, that's what she said: the early hours.'

'And he wouldn't come to your place, obviously, because then you wouldn't be sitting here asking me what you should do – would you?'

'No. He doesn't know where I am.'

'Well would he have any way of finding out?' Sharmini prods the nettles with a wooden spoon, sighs, closes the lid and returns to the table.

'I don't think so. They say they don't give out addresses because it just makes things difficult for them.'

'Mm. You know what this reminds me of?'

'No.'

'Those riddles from a few years ago. You know: "A man is

lying dead on the floor. Next to him is a stick and a pile of sawdust under a chair. There's another man looking in through the window laughing. Why is he laughing?"'

'Why does it remind you of that?'

'Sometimes you have to puzzle things out a bit – but when you get the answer you can't understand why you didn't work it out straight away.'

Jane hears a sound behind her and when she looks around Colonel Ovkis is standing just inside the kitchen door. He lifts the lid on his biscuit tin, reaches inside, and takes out a thin hand-rolled cigarette which he puts to his lips.

'Do you have a light, please?' he asks Sharmini. He is careful to give each word equal weight as if offence would be caused to the others if he did not. She hands him her lighter, which he strikes expertly before leaving the room trailing a cloak of exotic smoke.

'He's so tight, he won't even buy a box of matches,' Sharmini whispers. 'They say he came over in the back of a lorry as an illegal – but that doesn't explain the car. He's even got a disabled sticker on it. I think he stole the badge from Mordecai's three-wheeler when some yobs turned it upside down with him in it. The fire brigade had to come because he couldn't get out. Too fat and one of his legs is wonky. He lives behind the kebab take-away. The council put ramps in.'

'Who does?'

'Mordecai. At least it was a kebab place until the health people closed it down.'

'. . . So why was he laughing?' Jane asks.

'He wasn't laughing. Would you be if you were trapped upside down in a cripple-car?'

'No. The man outside the room in the puzzle.'

'Because he was the second smallest man in the world.'

'I don't understand.'

'And the man inside was the smallest man in the world, but the man outside cut his measuring stick and he thought he'd grown so he killed himself. So now the man outside was the smallest man in the world. That's why he was laughing.'

'How could he see through the window?'

'I don't think that comes into it. I expect it was a low window. Or he was standing on a crate.'

'. . . I suppose Billy might have found out where I was living from the social-work people.'

'I doubt it. But he might go back to where you lived before.'

'He wouldn't know the address.'

'It's amazing what you do know. I fell over in the snow and I was less than two years old and it seems like yesterday.'

'I've just remembered,' Jane says.

'What?'

'Why I went back in. It was all to do with John.'

'Well I could have told you that. It's always to do with him.'

'He's dead.'

'Is he? . . . Well I wish I could say I was sorry but I think he probably got what he deserved . . . but I am sorry. For you.'

'They found him in a wood. He'd been hit over the head.'
And as Jane begins to tell the story she remembers the
drawer in which she keeps his mementoes, and from there
it is a short distance to the notes that he left for her, and the
notes she wrote for him. '. . . My God,' Jane says. 'I know
where he's gone!'

'You see. You just had to puzzle it through.'

'I left Billy an address. In a bar of chocolate – but it was
ages ago. Ages!'

'That's where he'll be, I expect.'

'Thank you.' Jane kisses the Sugar Plum Fairy on her
powdery cheek. 'Thank you so much!'

'Where are you going?'

'I'm going to find him.'

'Ask the Colonel to drive you – I'm sure he won't mind.'

'I couldn't.'

'He won't mind.' Sharmini is standing now, preparing for
action. 'Be a bit flirty with him. I'll come with you if you
like. You might have to lend me some money for some
ciggies. I'll just have a wee before we go.'

'I don't know. I think it might frighten Billy if we all
turned up.'

'Well, we'll wait outside. Come on. I might get away
without having to make the supper.'

'I need to go home first and get changed.'

'That's all right. The Colonel won't mind. He likes a nice
drive out of an evening.'

*

Jane and Sharmini are sitting in the back seat of Colonel Ovkis's Humber Sceptre. He is alone in the front with his biscuit tin on the passenger seat. The leather seats are scuffed and some of the springs have gone, but, as Sharmini comments each time they go around a bend, it is a remarkably comfortable ride. To Jane's annoyance she waves regally each time they pass a bus queue; her greetings are met by walls of stony faces. Jane's anxiety over Billy's welfare, which had subsided during the conversation in Sharmini's kitchen, has now returned. She is certain of very little of what lies ahead of her but about one thing she is sure: she does not want the Sugar Plum Fairy anywhere near Billy and her mother and father when she meets them.

In the driving mirror she catches sight of Colonel Ovkis's glittering eyes trained on her. He had readily agreed to drive them after a whispered conversation with Sharmini; Jane has a terrible feeling that a promise has been made which she will have to deliver on later. They have already stopped for cigarettes, which Jane was obliged to pay for with her last ten-pound note, and once they were in the newsagent's, Sharmini had said that it would be a nice gesture to buy the Colonel some chocolates too for his trouble. Her change was therefore put towards a box of Quality Street which, having remained clamped between Sharmini's knees since then, has now been surreptitiously opened.

'It's just round here,' Jane says. 'Turn left after the bookshop and I'm at the end of the road.'

The Colonel nods with the economical courtesy of a chauffeur.

'What did you say to him?' Jane whispers to Sharmini.

'Don't worry about it,' she says, opening her fifth chocolate.

'I am worried about it.'

'I might have led him to believe he'd see some kissykissy action. That's all.'

Hearing a word he recognizes, the Colonel winks at Sharmini, and the speed of the old car picks up.

'He's driving too fast,' Jane says. 'There are kids round here.'

'Slow down, Colonel. Her ladyship doesn't want you killing any of the local children.'

'Look. This has been very kind of you, but I think it would be better if I went on my own.'

'Next left. LEFT!' Sharmini shouts and the car slews around the corner into Jane's road. Seeing the two women sandwiched together against the door, the Colonel smiles and nods in encouragement.

'It's too late, dear,' Sharmini says. 'We're nearly there now, and the Colonel's not going to just go away without his reward. Anyway, I've always wanted to see your place.'

'Don't you understand?' Jane says. 'I don't have time for you to come and see my place. I'm going to find my son who's gone missing.'

'He's not going to go anywhere, Jane. Don't go getting your knickers in a knot. You're always such a drama queen. Another hour or so won't make any difference.'

'An hour for what?'

'You know,' Sharmini says. 'What I promised the Colonel.'

'That's it. Let me out here.' Jane says, reaching for the door handle. She has now remembered why they argued outside the hospital: the Sugar Plum Fairy was always trying to take over her life. Twice she has resisted her, the last time by running away under the pretence of using the toilet. And now she curses herself for having allowed herself to forget what the other woman was capable of.

The Colonel does not stop the car so Jane pulls the handle and the door opens. Beneath her the road rushes by in a grey blur. She can see the tyres of the parked cars they're passing and short bursts of double yellow lines in the gaps between the vehicles. Just as she is about to throw herself out, the road slows down and soon stops altogether. Jane climbs out in silence sensing the disappointment and disapproval of the Sugar Plum Fairy. She closes the door without looking back at her.

As she dashes towards the house, Jane fumbles in her bag for her front door key, but as she reaches the door she hears somebody running along the street in her direction. She pauses, frozen, the key in the lock, as the footsteps slow behind her and then stop. She is too afraid to look around. She has no energy left to repel the Sugar Plum Fairy. If she and the Colonel gang up on her she'll just have to get it over with as quickly as possible. But the voice she hears is a man's.

'It's all right.' The voice is gentle and soothing and Jane

immediately recognizes it. She doesn't turn, but feels Patrick's firm hand on her back, gently guiding her around to face him.

25

Jane changes hurriedly. Her bedroom door is open and through it she is conducting a halting conversation with Patrick who is waiting in the living room. He had spotted her getting out of the Colonel's car and had immediately known she was in trouble.

'. . . Anyway,' Jane concludes. 'I thought I'd have to jump out of the car but the Colonel stopped so I didn't have to hurt myself.' She zips her perfumed body into the dress she has chosen for her reconciliation with Billy. She discarded her first and second choices. The first because somehow she knew her mother would disapprove – the hem was too short. The second because she felt it made her look too frumpish. Her third choice was a simple, violet, cotton dress the simplicity of which sets off her beauty and seems to cling to her as if her body had been used for the mannequin. When she bought it from the charity shop she had been so nervous that they had got the price wrong that she'd bundled it into a ball before thrusting it onto the counter. She'd even refused the offer of a plastic bag for it. But once she was outside the shop she had straightened it and laid it over her arm, then taken it around to the dry-cleaner's. She had not worn it since she'd collected it and had to strip the thin cellophane skin from it to remove it from the hanger. She knew she would never need to ask how she looked in that dress, although she was aware that when she did ask such questions it was only because she was seeking reassurance, never approval. She slipped on her 'Molly' shoes because they complemented the dress perfectly.

Jane wondered what Hackett's reaction would be; whether, with all the time gone by, he would be able to see her as his daughter again, or whether he would only ever see her as the woman he had made her. Except he had only half made her, and she knew the distance between the two was the journey she would be taking for the rest of her life. She hoped, as she looked in the mirror and turned first to her left and then to her right, that the confusion she felt over Hackett wasn't part of the same feeling she had about Billy. For him she just wanted to look nice so he'd be proud of her; whatever had gone wrong over the past ten years, she had never taken Billy into that awful dark place that Hackett had led her to.

'Well!' Patrick says when she walks into the room. He is

standing by the window and had been peering out at the street.

'Do you like it?'

'Give us a twirl.'

Patrick takes Jane's hand, holds it above her head and she turns a full circle. When she is facing him again he releases her hand; while they were touching she felt as though they were sharing the same body.

'I could drive you,' Patrick says. 'I'm sure Fergal would lend me his car.'

'No. I need to go on my own.'

'Are you ready for this?' Patrick takes Jane's hand again.

'I don't know. Tell me what I need to do.'

'I can't tell you that.'

'I don't know whether I should feel happy or sad.'

'Don't worry what you should be feeling. Just try and feel it.'

'I can't.'

Patrick smiles.

'What?' Jane asks him.

'Wouldn't it be great just to . . . Sometimes I look at Fergal when he's ranting or raving or when he's standing in a club and talking and it's like, it's obvious that what he's saying is really annoying the person he's talking to but he doesn't notice. He just doesn't see it. Wouldn't it be great to be like that?'

'Yes,' Jane says. But she doesn't know if she agrees or not. She doesn't want to hear about Fergal tonight. She wants to have some time alone with Patrick so she can pretend they have a future together; a nice flat with tall windows and long white curtains that drag on the beautiful wooden floors, and lovely furniture, and a garden so that Billy can go outside and play with his toys without her having to worry about him running out onto the road. In this life together they would never get old, and Billy would be frozen at the age he was before anybody from the outside world got hold of him and took him away and tried to tell him things he didn't need to know.

'Well, I suppose you'd better be off,' Patrick says. To his credit, he has picked up on Jane's impatience. 'It's getting late. Got everything?'

'Yes.' Jane looks around the flat as she collects her bag from the arm of the settee. Patrick goes to the door and holds it open for her to walk through, but at the last moment she stops and takes another look around the room.

'You go on,' she says. 'I just need some time on my own.' She kisses his cheek because it seems like the most natural thing to do.

'You take care.'

'I will. Thank you, Patrick.'

When Patrick has left, Jane goes to her memento drawer. She opens it, closes her eyes, and rummages inside. Her hand finds a cold, metal lighter. It was the one *he* used for lighting the candles and his occasional cigarette which he always insisted on smoking half-hanging out of the window (even though she said she didn't mind a bit of smoke in the room). Why did he have to leave her? Why doesn't the pain of a lost love like that just go away with time? When she thinks of him Jane still feels that quickening of her heart, that tightening of her chest, as if it was yesterday. Perhaps I'm not mad, she thinks. Perhaps I'm the sanest person in the world – because surely sanity is feeling things deeply and showing what you're feeling straight away. She used to know how to do that. So did the Sugar Plum Fairy. She used to call her tablets her delayers and when Jane asked her why, she said it was because they didn't make her better, they just delayed the time when she would have to deal with her problems.

'Goodbye, darling,' Jane says, as she closes the door on her flat. But there is no reply.

When Alf comes to the door Jane can see that, like Patrick, he approves of her dress. He takes a step back so that he can look at it, shakes his head in wonder and says: 'Blimey.'

'I'm going out,' Jane says.

'Somewhere nice?'

'I hope so.'

'Well, you take care walking around the streets looking like that. Have you got a coat?'

'Yes.' Jane leans towards Alf and kisses him on the cheek.

'What was that for?' he asks her.

'I'm sorry for all the horrible things I've said and all the horrible things I've done.'

'What brought all this on?'

'Nothing in particular.'

'. . . You look after yourself.'

They embrace and Jane leaves trying not to look back along the corridor towards Maude's and the flat that Frankie shares with Carey and, sometimes at the weekends, The Boy. She can't resist it though, and when she turns she sees Alf waving goodbye as she goes down the stairs.

26

Billy is wallowing in the biggest bath he's ever been in. Only now does he understand why old people prefer baths to showers: because when you lie down flat and your body is covered by water at the right temperature, you feel as though you are connected to the world in a different way. It's almost the same feeling you get at the swimming baths, but there, when you stop moving about, you soon get cold. When you wee it warms your legs but a moment later you're colder than you were before.

The food in his stomach is also adding to his sense of well-being. He couldn't finish the fish and chips his Nan had presented him with even though they were the best fish and chips he had ever eaten. But it wasn't just the taste he liked, it was the fact that he was able to eat without the feeling of anxiety that usually cramped his stomach. He noticed it only because it had diminished. As he lies in the water he can hear the television in the background; it is no louder than conversation. At Fiona and Don's house he rarely watched TV because Fiona wouldn't let him have it loud enough. In the home where he stayed before that, it was on so loudly that it always gave him a headache. Here, at his Nan and Granddad's, it was just right. He is sorry not to have met the grumpy old man and the thin old woman before because they really do seem to like him; neither of them stared at him as if they expected anything of him or disapproved of him. At Don and Fiona's he was never sure what it was he was supposed to be doing. All he knew was that it wasn't what he was doing at that particular moment. Don was as bad in that respect as Fiona. With Don it was usually some-thing to do with the way he cut up his food, the amount he put into his mouth, and the number of times he chewed. With Fiona it was everything else: how he sat on the settee with his trainers on, the way she said he clumped about the house all the time and the fact that he made his clothes dirty just by wearing them. She also accused him of not taking enough showers, but when he did she would knock on the door after five minutes to tell him not to use up all the hot water. And then, afterwards, she would moan if he put the wet towels in the laundry basket because they were wet – and if he put them in the airing cupboard she'd complain that he hadn't folded them up properly.

'Are you all right, Billy?' he hears. It is his Nan. 'Nan.' He likes saying the word to himself because it feels as comfortable as a warm towel. The associations of it are all new and untainted. 'Granddad' feels different but no less safe: Granddad might be grumpy, but he'd never mean it and you'd know that Nan would be there to tell him to cheer up. The only thing that spoils it all for him is the question he doesn't feel able to ask: why he has never seen them before? He knows that something terrible must have happened between them and his mother, and it must have been dreadful for her never to have mentioned it. But he can't imagine either of them being capable of doing a terrible thing. So perhaps his mother did the awful thing and they sent her away as a punishment. Thinking of his mother and the people she has hurt, his anxiety floods back.

'Billy? Do you need your towel yet?'

'Yes please.' Billy doesn't feel embarrassed when his Nan pushes the door open, comes in and stands looking down at him in the water.

'You're very thin, I must say,' she says, holding the towel wide, inviting him to stand and step out of the bath so that she can drape it around him. Billy takes the sides of the metal bath and lifts himself to his feet. He is careful to step onto the towelling mat and not to get the floor wet. His Nan then swaddles the towel around him and folds it over itself at his back so that his arms are pinned to his side. While she pats him dry they stand as close as if they were dancing, both enjoying the proximity. Billy can see the deep lines in her face and a thin layer of milky film over the faded blue of her eyes and it makes him sad that she is very old and he has

231

only just met her. He is so close that he could easily kiss her on the cheek, and he wonders if he did whether her face would feel like skin or paper.

'There, you'd better finish yourself off.' His Nan steps back but she doesn't seem to want to leave the room and Billy doesn't mind her standing there as he dries himself between his toes, tugs the towel around his shoulders, and then pats down his own chest.

'I don't suppose you bought any pyjamas did you?' she asks him.

'Yes. And some socks and pants.'

'You are grown-up aren't you? I'll fetch your bag.'

As Billy sits on the lavatory he catches sight of a blurred image of himself in the misted-up mirror. He puts on his glasses and wipes the mirror clean: he seems older than he remembers he looked, last time he really noticed himself, but without his clothes on he feels a bit like a baby. When his Nan returns with his bag he is glad when she leaves him alone to put his pyjamas on: she seems to sense his feelings, and that's another thing he likes about her.

When he is dressed he folds the towel over the side of the bath and reaches in to pull out the plug. The water is deeper than it looks and he wets his cuff. The plug is stiff and when he pulls it out a bubble burps from the plughole. The water doesn't seem to be going down very quickly and he wonders if the drain is blocked, but after he has been watching for a few minutes he can see it has dropped below the ring of dirt on the bath. Behind the toilet he finds a stiff cloth and a yellow plastic container of bath cleaner. He squirts a line of yellow cream above the ring of dirt, drops the cloth into the bathwater to bring it back to life and then rubs the bath clean in the way Fiona showed him.

When the water is almost all gone he can see a tiny typhoon going down into the plughole and he watches it as the remains of his bath are funnelled away into the drain. He then picks up his clothes and goes into the lounge where Hackett is watching the television. His Nan is busy in the kitchen.

'Do you watch this?' Hackett says, gesturing towards the screen. 'She likes it, but I can't be bothered with it.' Nevertheless, he goes on staring at the television.

The programme is not one Billy knows; a medical drama in which a nurse is talking to an old man in a hospital cubicle. The man looks at the nurse's breasts as she plumps up his pillows and straightens his sheets under his chin. A machine bleeps beside him.

'Bloody stupid if you ask me. . . I've told her to smoke in the kitchen,' Hackett says after a pause. 'It stinks in here. Bad for your chest . . . good bath?'

'Yes.'

'I don't know what she's doing in there.' Hackett cranes around in his chair and calls, 'What are you doing in there?'

'I'm making a cup of tea.'

'Your show's on.'

'What time is it?'

'Nearly ten.'

'You've upset her routine,' Hackett says to Billy. 'What time do you go to bed?'

'Any time.'

'What – you stay up all night, do you?'

'No.'

'When then?'

'Nine-thirty. Or ten o'clock.'

'And what do you get up to until then?'

'Play on my X-Box.'

'X what?'

'It's a games console.'

'Is it indeed?'

'Yes.'

'. . . So you're not staying with your mother then?'

'No.'

'Is she . . .? These people you stay with – all right, are they?'

'All right.'

'Would you say they adopted you?'

'Not yet. They want to. But when I'm eighteen I can leave.'

'And that's what you want, is it?'

'Yes.'

'Leave and go where?'

'To my mum.'

'Right.'

'. . . Cup of tea, Billy?'

Billy looks around, sensing that his Nan has been standing at the door for some time.

'No thank you,' he says.

'You're a very polite boy, I must say.'

'Too polite,' Hackett says.

'Nothing wrong with that. Manners are useful.'

'Not in this world.'

'Can I get you anything?'

'No thank you.'

'Look. You've missed your show now,' Hackett says as the theme tune comes on.

'Turn it off.'

'I'm waiting for the news.'

'He likes his news.'

'I like to keep up with what's going on.'

'. . . So what do you watch Billy?'

'Cartoons. Takeshi's Castle.'

'Do you like the cinema?' Hackett asks.

'Yes.'

'We used to go to the flicks, didn't we?'

'Every week . . . I expect there's things you might want to ask us, is there?' his Nan says.

Billy shakes his head gently.

'I think he just wants some peace and quiet now,' Hackett says. 'Eh? Bit of peace and quiet?'

Billy doesn't know what to say to that so he smiles but it doesn't feel quite right because he feels he's hurting his Nan by doing it. She smiles back at him to show him that she doesn't mind. Then there is nothing.

He wakes briefly as somebody guides his head onto a

pillow and drapes a sheet over him. The pillow smells familiar, as if he was lying back at home in his own bed, it belongs to the time before he got taken away in the car and he tried to be brave for his mother.

27

From the hot, upper deck of the bus Jane sleepily watches the streets go past. It is eleven-thirty but the shops remain lit. A crowd of men refused entrance to a club have gathered on the pavement outside Woolworths; one is attempting to climb onto the shoulders of another, a third is trying to help him up but he is drunk and they all end up sprawling on their backs on the ground. One stands up and gives a hefty kick to the armour-plated glass of the shop door.

'Prats,' says the man sitting behind Jane.

'They're just having a bit of fun,' Jane hears from the woman sitting with him, her voice slurred by Bacardi Breezers.

'You don't have to pick up the pieces.'

'Don't you have fun ever?' the woman asks.

'Yeah. But I know my limits – and my idea of fun doesn't involve going round kicking the crap out of private property.'

Spotting a Poundsaver shop ahead of them, Jane stands up and rings the bell on the silver pole. The journey seems to have taken her hours. She has changed bus twice; the second time she'd done so, she'd had to wait for half an hour in a cold bus station, where she tried to keep away from a drunken woman who was pestering her for change.

Jane has been back here before. Like a prisoner planning a break-out she has familiarized herself with the landmarks – but she has never before found the courage to knock on the door of the house she shared with Hackett and her mother all those years ago. The closest she got was when she pushed the jungle photograph through the letterbox. Why she had felt compelled to do that, she still didn't really know. If, on one of those visits, she had seen her mother on the street she wouldn't have known what to say to her. If she had encountered Hackett she would have been shy and afraid. Tonight she knows she will have no choice but to confront them; without the excuse of Billy being there she would never have found the courage. Billy is her soldier, her saviour, her strength. When the bus turns into the familiar road, she knows she will have to trust her instincts and hopes that they don't let her down as they have done, so often in the past.

Standing in the cold street, watching the fairground-bright bus sail away into the night Jane is chilly and dizzy. She tries to remember when she last ate and realizes it must have been the previous day because that day's toast had been thrown into the bin by the policewoman. She allows herself a moment of self-pity, but then, as always, finds herself instead grieving over the loss of her son.

'You should like yourself more,' the Sugar Plum Fairy once suggested to her.

'I do.'

'You don't.'

The Sugar Plum Fairy had been filing her nails. They had found a closed ward at the back of the hospital which was being used to store old beds, a huge light from an operating theatre and a number of screens. The room was full of ghosts. It creaked when they sat silently. Sometimes they heard footsteps and they would cling to each other until they stopped. Once they went there at night but they were too afraid to stay; the Sugar Plum Fairy said she could hear the spirits communing and they shouldn't disturb them.

They had found some old rest-room chairs and made a den at the centre of the ward inside a maze of grey screens. Nobody seemed to mind that they disappeared for hours on end as long as they turned up for the group therapy sessions.

'You seem to think you know everything about me,' Jane said. 'But you don't.'

'You're an open book to everybody but yourself. Well, you are to me anyway. I should have been a psychiatrist.'

'It can't be that hard I expect.'

'Of course it's not. Everybody's the same. Bonkers or not.

It's not rocket science. There's only a few pills that work and you soon find out whether they do or not.'

'Well if you're so clever, why are you in here?' Jane felt strong that day: she hadn't slept very well and her mind was racing.

'Because I'm unconventional and society finds that threatening.'

'Anyway, I do like myself.' Jane wanted the Sugar Plum Fairy to finish what she had been saying. Sometimes she felt she learned more about herself from her than from the doctors.

'You're pretty. People like you don't have to try as hard as the rest of us. Really beautiful people get by without any personality at all.'

'So what are you saying?'

'I'm saying that you don't like yourself. But you do fancy yourself. And that's quite dangerous. Me, I'm sensitive to the needs of others. I've had to work on my personality because I know that I'm not the most beautiful woman in the world. But I am beautiful inside. Usually.'

'How do you make yourself beautiful inside?'

'By ignoring all your natural inclinations; thinking the best of people instead of the worst. Closing your eyes to people being selfish and telling yourself they can't help it. Doing things for people even when you don't want to. Never passing judgement. Not hating people who deserve to be hated. Believing that people can be saved. Especially that. And I think if you really believe it it works like a magic spell.'

'How?'

'I'm not sure yet – I'm still working through some of my issues.'

The old familiar house seems to know Jane. It looks down upon her sternly, but she doesn't feel it is judging her or pushing her away. The night is quiet save for the occasional passing car and a brief burst of barking from a dog demanding to be let back into the warm.

Seeing the note taped over the broken bell, Jane knocks on the door but the timid echo is swallowed in the cavernous hallway. She sees the hole in the door-glass and reaches through it into the chilly air inside. She feels for the catch of the lock. It twists easily and the huge door swings inwards.

Once inside the hallway something makes her turn and look back towards the stained glass of the door; the angle she is viewing it from is wrong. She knows she must climb the stairs and sit on the third tread. She does. Now she is home. This is where she perched waiting for Hackett to return from work with his armful of presents, his long cigarette clamped between his lips, his tie loosened and his beautiful, silver-grey coat billowing out behind him. And, on the rare occasions when he had had a really good day, he'd take a wad of money from his back pocket and throw it up in the air and it would shower down over them as he danced around the hallway with her in his arms. On those nights Jane knew that everything would be all right because her mother and father wouldn't argue about money. Hackett would go down to the off-licence for a bottle of gin, two bottles of wine, one of tonic water, and a tin of nuts. And when he came back he would toss her the nuts and let her pop open the tin, so she would be the only one privileged to smell the woody air trapped inside. Her parents would drink most of the gin while her mother tried to cook, and then they would open the wine. Usually on those nights they wouldn't have anything to eat because before the food was ready Hackett and her mother would end up in the bedroom and that would be the last she saw of them for the night. Jane would make herself bread and jam and watch the television until it was past her bedtime. Then she would put herself to bed, always remembering to clean her teeth first. It was a question her mother always asked her when she emerged blearily from the bedroom in the morning: had she cleaned her teeth? Once Jane had made the mistake of telling her she had not, which had earned her several smacks on her head. She knew it was the guilt her mother felt that made her lash out, but knowing the reason made it none the less painful.

Jane touches the stair beside her. The carpet is gone. The wood feels rough and dusty. Once the Edwardian building must have represented wealth and elegance because Hackett and her mother did – at one time – have money. When Jane was born they owned the whole house. But then, when Hackett lost his car lot, they began renting out rooms. First, an old merchant seaman called Gerald Bliss moved into the back room on the ground floor. Then the whole top floor was taken by a Pakistani man who said he was bringing his family over. Something happened and they never arrived. After he disappeared, leaving his clothes and an old gas mask behind packed neatly in a cardboard box, a noisy Greek man arrived with a woman who spoke no English and her three timid children. After that Hackett sold off the basement to a young couple and soon Jane's family were just like everybody else in there, restricted to their own small part of the house.

Jane stands and climbs the stairs to the top. The first thing she notices when she reaches the hallway is that the lampshade has gone and a single bulb dangles from the ceiling on a long flex. The wattage is low and the light it gives off is miserly. Billy is close now. She can sense him. She wants to cry but she stops herself.

Where would he be? Where would her mother have made up a bed for him? He wouldn't sleep in their room like she had done until they banished her to the tiny room by the kitchen. For the first time a doubt crosses her mind: what if Billy isn't there? What if he arrived and they didn't take him in. She had made a number of assumptions: that they would recognize Billy, that they would welcome him in, and that Billy would be happy to stay with them. Well, why not? Why shouldn't something turn out the way she had planned, for a change?

Billy would be in the living room. That's where he would be. If she tapped on the door then perhaps she could wake him without alerting Hackett and her mother.

A new plan formulates in her mind. She could wake Billy and take him away without having to see her mother and father and go through the terrible agony of it all. But surely that was the whole point of it. She had sent Billy here rather than to her own flat for a reason: because . . . because . . . But she can't remember why. She had been a bit mad when she gave him the chocolate and now couldn't make all the connections she had made then. Her mad mind is a frozen lake. When it thaws she can no longer walk across the ice to the island of understanding.

She knocks three times. After a pause the door opens slowly and she is confronted by an old woman clasping her blue dressing gown tightly at the base of her neck. Her knuckles are large and arthritic; her skin is glossy and tight.

Jane can immediately see that age has changed her mother. Sometimes, Jane knows, it has a habit of doing that to you. If you learn as you grow and hold onto your strength, you earn the right to become the person you deserve to be. If you don't, you have to take the personality the world throws at you. Her mother's only chance would have been to leave Hackett, but they believed they needed each other and they probably did; conjoined twins sharing a pair of lungs and one, small, shrivelled heart.

'Hello,' Jane says, stopping short of adding 'Mummy', 'Mum' or 'Mother', none of which seems right. Neither woman feels inclined to travel the small distance that remains between them.

'You take after him. People used to say you looked like me.'

Jane is surprised by the slight poshness in the old woman's voice. She had forgotten about her mother's airs and graces and how Hackett was always taking the mickey out of her because of them. In looking like Hackett, Jane has already disappointed her, and then she remembers that she was always a disappointment to her mother.

'Is Billy here?' Jane asks, trying to keep the regret from her voice. In real life there are rarely the moments of revelation that you see on the television. The best you can hope for is that afterwards, when you're puzzling it through, you can put another piece of the jigsaw in place. Jane decides that perhaps the Sugar Plum Fairy had the right idea: perhaps we're all looking through a window at a dwarf lying dead by a chair and trying to understand what it means.

'We put him in the lounge.' Her mother, for the first time, seems unsure of herself. Billy is the fragile commodity that has been entrusted into her care. Did she do the right thing by letting him sleep on the settee?

'Is he all right?'

'We had fish and chips. It was Hackett's idea.'

Hearing the name, Jane blushes, and her mother pretends not to notice. She steps aside, pressing her back against the wall and Jane passes her and goes into the living room. When her eyes adjust to the light she sees the shape of Billy on the settee, the top of his head just visible over the upholstered arm. Jane goes to him and kneels beside him. She pulls the cover down from his face and looks into his sleeping face. His breath is sweet and fishy and she welcomes it against her cheek. She brushes his forehead gently with her lips and it feels like she is kissing her own hand. He opens his eyes and then closes them again. Jane feels a pain in her knees; her joints are cramped, but she is grateful for the pain because it reminds her who she is and why she is here.

'Let him sleep,' Jane hears from her mother. It is no more than a suggestion and Jane recognizes that Billy has given her a power she'd never had before. Perhaps that's why she posted the jungle photograph through the door – to show she now had something her parents would recognize as being of value. If she damaged her son it would hurt them, and that's where her new power lay.

She doesn't stand immediately, and when she does she looks at her mother in such a way as to show her that she had done it because she wanted to and not because her mother had suggested it.

'What do you want to do?' her mother says, no longer making any pretence at warmth.

'I'd like a drink. In the kitchen.'

Her mother leads the way and waits just inside the kitchen door for Jane to follow her in. Only when she has pulled the door shut does she turn on the light and take the opportunity to look her daughter up and down.

'You've got a good figure, Jane. Not too thin. I don't like seeing these girls too thin. I don't know why they think they need to show their belly buttons off all the time.'

'It's the fashion.'

'I can't see you going round showing off your stomach to all and sundry.'

'I don't. It's just young girls.'

'Some of them aren't so young.'

They wait, and as the tension evaporates Jane asks. 'When did Billy get here?'

'A few hours ago. Late this afternoon.'

'How does he seem?'

'He's a lovely lad.'

'I know.'

'. . . Do you want tea?'

'No.'

'We told him. About being his grandparents. I hope that was all right.'

'Up to you.'

'It was Hackett who realized.'

'And what did Billy say when you told him?'

'He asked, did that mean that he could stay?'

'So he wanted to stay?'

'Yes. He wants to see you.'

'Did he say that?'

'Yes. He misses you.'

Jane sits down heavily on the kitchen chair. All she now wants to do is sleep. She can't remember the last time she slept properly. Certainly it was before she started taking the tablets. The sleep they induce is shallow; making her feel as if she's being held down by firm hands. When she wakes she has to fight to get out of their clutches and for an hour or so afterwards she feels groggy. But she has left her tablets at home. She'll have to take them tomorrow. One night won't hurt without them.

'I'm tired,' Jane says.

'Will you stay here tonight?'

'I don't know.'

'Well, do you have anywhere else to go?'

'I could go home. With Billy.'

'He's settled. Why don't you leave him tonight.' Her mother approaches her and tentatively places a hand on Jane's shoulder. 'You need some rest . . . we can talk in the morning.'

Jane feels herself drawn by her mother's proximity. Her mother moves closer and Jane rests her head against her. A door in her head opens and she goes to a place where she is happy and unafraid. Jane knows she has a greater claim to this place at her mother's breast than anybody else in the world. Even Hackett had to relinquish his claim on her mother's breasts when she was born. Jane can feel the soft juddering beat of her mother's heart as she breathes in the detergent fragrance of her dressing gown.

'I'm sorry,' Jane hears from her mother.

Regret, as Jane well knows, is easy. But she wonders if now she will get the answer to the question the doctors were always asking her: 'Why do you think your parents sent you away?'

She could solve the puzzle for Hackett. She would say that she hoped that he'd suddenly seen what he was doing to her and some shred of decency in him made him do it to protect her from him. But her mother – she could never really figure that one out. Her mother was cruel and insecure and she couldn't really look after herself, but there was never any doubt that she loved her. And she must have loved her a great deal to send her away. She must have had a terrible amount of love for her.

'We'll stay here tonight,' Jane says.

'Good.'

'I'd like to go to sleep now.' Jane pulls away from her mother's warmth. 'I'll sleep in a chair in the lounge. If that's all right.'

While her mother goes to the bedroom to find a blanket, Jane tugs a chair close to the settee, locates Billy's hand inside the warmth of the sheets and holds it tight. When her mother returns to the lounge Jane is asleep, sitting upright in the chair, holding Billy's hand. She doesn't stir when the blanket is wrapped around her.

Then, from the bedroom door, Hackett emerges, tying the shiny crimson rope of his dressing gown. Jane's mother shakes her head, indicating that he must not wake his daughter. But Hackett has no intention of waking Jane. His wife is watching him, trying to hate him but she can't. She never could. There was always something magnificent about her husband: a man who rose above the circumstances of his brutal upbringing, who came to her with an edge and a passion and a nervy, infectious appetite for the world. But underneath it there was nothing but fear. He had nothing and therefore he had nothing to lose. Though it never stopped him trying to exert his power over the world. And when Jane had come along there was someone he had unquestioned power over because he had created her.

She remembers what attracted her to Hackett at the beginning: it was his ridiculous bravado. And that was what saved him when she discovered what he was doing to their daughter.

Jane wakes. Billy's hand is still in hers. When she sees Hackett she's shocked because all that is left of him is an old man with thick, grey hair, a cadaverous face, and eyes that look as if they have seen too much. Jane is glad that her face does not burn with shame when she sees his reaction to her dress. She feels a guilty pleasure at knowing now why she chose to wear it.

'Hello Janey, love,' he says in a broken voice from a used-up heart.

She turns away to show him that she doesn't belong to him any more. She belongs to Billy. Billy, whom she made without any help from him or her mother. It wasn't her fault he was taken away from her. She did her best. And now the boy has woken and is whispering to her.

'Has he woken up?' Hackett says, embarrassed by the accusations hanging in the silence.

'It's all right, love,' Jane soothes her son. She leans down and hears Billy say something about chocolate: a chocolate wrapper.

'I only found it this week,' he tells her.

'You got here. I'm very proud of you.'

'He came on his own. Fair distance too,' Hackett tells her. 'We had fish and chips.'

'I know,' Jane says. 'She told me.'

'I wanted to take him to the pub but your mother said we should eat here.'

'Sit down, Hackett, you'll make yourself dizzy,' Jane's mother says.

'Right,' Hackett says and obeys. He watches the women, waiting for a signal as to what he should do next. If Jane didn't want to make conversation with him it was up to her. She was always a feisty one, was Janey.

The covers slip from Billy's feet and Jane reaches out and tenderly touches his beautiful toes. His nails, she is sad to see, need cutting. She can feel her mother standing in solidarity behind her. Billy sits up on the settee. As Jane relinquishes his hand there is a distant knock on the front door and her heart stops. Past midnight. It can only mean one thing. Only trouble knocks after midnight.

'Are you all right, Billy?' Jane asks him. She knows they don't have too long now.

'Yes. Are you all right?'

'I am now.'

'Who's that knocking at this time of night?' Hackett says. But they all knew it couldn't last. Jane and Billy belong in other places now, and the authorities have come to take them away and put them back.

'Go and get dressed,' Jane whispers, and Billy, glad of any

251

instruction, takes his pile of clothes to the bathroom, closing the door behind him.

'I'll put the kettle on,' Jane's mother says.

'I wouldn't bother,' Hackett tells her.

There is another knock on the front door. Billy hears it through the bathroom door. As he dresses he watches a spider weaving a web in the corner of the ceiling. He tries to hear what his mother is saying to his granddad, hoping that it might give him a clue as to why he hasn't met them before, but neither of them are speaking. He knew the visit would have to end, but he's sad that the end has had to come so soon. In the brief time in which he had shared the company of the only three people in the world he belongs to, he had tried to understand what it meant. He tried hard to feel what it was he didn't feel when he was with Don and Fiona. There was peace, and some hope for the future, but he didn't sense much love between his mother and his grandparents. In fact it had been better before his mother arrived. Since then, all the good feelings that seemed to be coming towards him bounced off as if he had a force-field around him.

When he is dressed, Billy emerges from the bathroom with his pyjamas folded in his arms.

'Come back,' Hackett is saying to his mother in a voice that is pitched too loud. 'Any time. Day or night. Both of you. We'd be very happy to see you here at any time.'

'Yes. I know,' Jane says. 'Come here.' She holds out her hand to Billy.

'Go,' Jane's mother says with a sudden urgency. 'You can get out the back way.'

'What?' Hackett says.

'Back way?'

'You've got your boy back. He's standing there. Look at him. This might be your only chance, Jane.'

'Might it?' Jane says weakly. 'Chance for what?' She looks towards Billy for reassurance. 'I just want what's best for Billy.'

But Billy doesn't know what's best for him and he feels it's unfair of them to ask him.

'There's no running,' Hackett says. 'You can never run far enough or fast enough. Go and get the front door.'

'Jane, is that what you want?'

And Jane knows that it is. She has done enough running and now she must leave. She has conducted herself well. It is already a source of pride to her that she didn't scream or shout or accuse them of all the things they did to her when she was young.

While Jane's mother goes to let the police in, Jane and Billy sit hand in hand on the settee. Hackett is now behind them, proudly standing guard over his family in his dressing gown.

28

For the first time in as long as she can remember, Jane doesn't mind waking when the sun is already up. Since she met Billy again there are still days when she finds it hard to get out of bed in the morning but there have been none when she has remained there all day. Patrick had stressed when he'd offered her the job at the bookshop café, that if it was too much for her, she must tell him and not make herself ill. Today is the first working day she has taken off since the bookshop re-opened three months ago; Patrick said she had earned some time away from making the coffee with his whizzy machine.

'It works, though, Jane,' Patrick had said, when she confided to him she was worried that people thought she was rude. Only occasionally could she think of anything to say when she handed the cup to the customer. The things she wanted to say, which came from her heart, didn't seem appropriate, although once a woman smiled when Jane told her she had a kind face.

'Stick to the weather, and, failing that, just smile,' Patrick advised. 'There's a great deal to be said for being enigmatic.'

'But I'm not enigmatic,' Jane had protested.

'Yes you are, my darling, you're the only truly enigmatic person I know.'

She had quickly mastered the Italian coffee machine. It was Patrick's real treasure and took pride of place in the top room of the bookshop. The books in there had all been cleared away, a wall had been taken down, a new wooden floor laid, windows put into the roof, and now it seemed like a proper café. Business was particularly good on Sundays when the young couples would come in and eat carrot cake and drowsily read the free newspapers spread about the low tables. They would sometimes lean against each other on the old settees, and most would drift away in the early afternoon. Jane liked watching them and imagined them returning home again to make love, or go to the pub to watch the Sunday afternoon football.

There was one boy who regularly came in alone. Before Patrick had even bothered to tease her about it, Jane knew that he was coming in to see her. She could have made it easy for him by offering a smile or a few words of encouragement. But she was in no hurry to go out for a drink with the shy boy who always wore black. She enjoyed the daily torture of wondering whether he was going to come and visit her. Patrick had warned her to be careful of him; he didn't trust the way his eyes kept shifting to the door whenever somebody new came in, and how he wouldn't meet your gaze. Nor did he like the fact that sometimes he saw a smile break over the boy's face for no apparent reason, or that occasionally he seemed to be talking to himself. The behaviour all seemed perfectly natural to Jane. She understood the shy boy completely.

The only uncertainty she had about her new life was Fergal. She knew on first meeting him that he didn't like her, but Patrick reassured her that the staff were his responsibility, not Fergal's and anyway, it was good for him to have something to be jealous of – it kept him on his toes. Fergal had a strange attitude when it came to Patrick and women: while he never felt any threat of losing him to another man, he was obsessed with a fear of losing him to a woman. Patrick and Jane spent many quiet afternoons discussing Fergal's insecurities, and Patrick seemed to enjoy the disloyalty of it.

'Perhaps he's seen something I haven't,' Patrick said, one wet afternoon. 'Perhaps, if the circumstances were right, I would fall for you.'

Jane had demurred, but she couldn't deny that the prospect of having Patrick to herself thrilled her. The sexual tension which grew between them made the days seem shorter and both of their lives more interesting.

Having risen late, and then taken a leisurely shower, Jane

caught the bus to the mall, where she is now waiting for Billy. It is raining outside, but the only indication of it in the perpetual daytime of the arcade is the slight humidity in the air. Jane is wearing a rain mac and has brought an umbrella with her. Having seen an old lady shaking hers out and then putting it up to dry on the floor beside her Jane does the same. She has bought herself a cup of cappuccino and she is drinking it slowly. Having become something of a connoisseur, she can tell that the beans were ground too long ago, and as a result the coffee is weak and stale. The milk, too, is slightly sour. She rolls a cigarette, one of the new indulgences she allows herself. Jane decided to take up smoking because she was fed up with people on the television telling her how bad it was for her. Feeling sorry for the tobacco companies, she decided to help them out.

Billy has not commented on her new habit. They have met twice since she went to fetch him from Hackett and her mother's flat. The meetings were organized by a new support worker, who Billy seemed to trust. So much so, in fact, that Jane was immediately jealous of her, which spoilt the first meeting because she ended up in tears of rage when the woman took Billy away. But then the woman returned to the table, leaving Billy waiting in the car. She talked to Jane for ten minutes and said things to her in a gentle tone of voice nobody had ever used with her before. When she went, Jane had been reassured that it had been all right to cry. Why shouldn't she feel jealous of another woman taking her son away? The second time they met the woman left her alone with Billy and they went out of the mall to a games arcade. While Billy played on one of the machines Jane stood behind him with a cup of coffee and a cigarette.

Today she has decided to ask the woman if she can take Billy to the cinema. She expects the woman will say no but, just in case, she has brought a local newspaper with her which has the cinema times in it. She has £20 in her purse which she estimates should be enough for two tickets, a drink for Billy, some popcorn and a bar of chocolate for him to take away with him.

She can see Billy coming now. He's chatting eagerly to the social-work woman, but when he catches sight of Jane his head drops a little and he stops talking. Jane is sorry to see him doing this, and she blames herself because she could see how much it had hurt Billy when she'd cried and lost her temper with the woman the time before last. But she knows she must learn from her mistakes and not dwell on them as she's done in the past. And she must forgive herself, because, as her new counsellor told her, she is not to blame. Sometimes Jane doesn't know what to say to the counsellor on her weekly visits because she leaves long pauses. But usually, if she waits without forcing herself to think of something, words just bubble to the surface and she finds herself chatting eagerly about all manner of things. Once they spent fifty minutes talking about sheep and going to farms and how important it was for children to spend time out in the open air. Afterwards she felt sad because she had only once taken Billy to a farm. But she didn't fight the sadness. She allowed it to come. Each time she cries now, Jane feels like she is draining a wound. Before, it was like screaming in the dark for her mother to come and lift her out of her cot and hold her tight.

Something Patrick told her comes into her mind as Billy and the woman approach her table. She had been worried for the future that day, and she had asked him why things couldn't turn out happily like they sometimes did in books. In reply, after giving the question serious consideration, Patrick had said to her that there were no happy endings, not in the proper books, because there are no happy endings in the real world. In fact, until you die, there are no endings at all. Just those occasional moments when you can pause, and take stock, and, if you're lucky, move on.

For news about current and forthcoming titles
from Portobello Books and for a sense of purpose
visit the website **www.portobellobooks.com**

encouraging voices,
supporting writers,
challenging readers

Portobello
BOOKS